FAMILY SECRETS

Art gallery owner Rhianna is shocked to receive a telephone call from a woman claiming to be her grandmother — someone she thought had died years ago. Her nerves aren't helped by the handsome stranger who has been acting suspiciously when visiting the gallery. Travelling to Brookhurst to investigate her new 'grandmother', Rhianna finds the very same stranger staying at her hotel. Is this a coincidence, or is he also tangled up in her family secrets . . . ?

Books by Jean M. Long
in the Linford Romance Library:

CORNISH RHAPSODY
THE MAN WITH GRANITE EYES
TO DREAM OF GOLD APPLES
ISLAND SERENADE
MUSIC OF THE HEART
BENEATH A LAKELAND MOON
JASMINE SUMMER
DESIGN FOR LOVING
RETURN TO HEATHERCOTE MILL
PICTURES OF THE PAST
THE GIFT OF LOVE
PROMISES OF SPRING

JEAN M. LONG

FAMILY
SECRETS

Complete and Unabridged

LINFORD
Leicester

First published in Great Britain in 2013

First Linford Edition
published 2014

A catalogue record for this book is available
from the British Library.

ISBN 978–1–4448–2080–5

Published by
F. A. Thorpe (Publishing)
Anstey, Leicestershire

Set by Words & Graphics Ltd.
Anstey, Leicestershire
Printed and bound in Great Britain by
T. J. International Ltd., Padstow, Cornwall

This book is printed on acid-free paper

1

Rhianna stared transfixed at the phone.

'I'm sorry, who did you say you were?' she asked the woman on the other end of the line, convinced that she must have misheard.

'Your grandmother, dear — Letitia Delroy.'

'My grandmother,' she repeated incredulously, 'then I'm afraid you must be mistaken. I don't have a grandmother.'

'Oh, but you do and I am she,' the elderly voice quavered insistently. 'As I've already said my name is Letitia Delroy — ring any bells?'

'No, I'm afraid not, although we certainly share the same surname. You see my grandparents died many years ago — before I was born.'

'So that's what your parents told you. And of course, you can't ask them, can you because they've both passed away now, haven't they?'

A tiny shiver ran down Rhianna's spine. 'How do you know that?' she asked.

'Because I'm your grandmother,' the elderly woman repeated patiently, as if she were speaking to a rather slow child.

Rhianna didn't like to put the phone down because it was obvious the woman needed to talk to someone.

'Why were you trying to get hold of me — I mean your granddaughter. Are you in some kind of trouble?' she asked gently.

There was a pause. 'I might be — there are certainly things going on here that I'm not happy about. Look, is there any chance of us meeting up? I'd really like to talk to you.'

'I — um — where are you?'

'I live in Kent. Look, I'll have to go now, but I'll be in touch again soon.'

Rhianna felt as if she had been having a particularly strange dream from which she was going to wake up at any moment.

'Your grandmother! If she'd said your sister or cousin it would have been more feasible!' Fiona Field exclaimed, leaving the picture she was hanging dangling precariously in mid-air. 'I bet it's a hoax — Marcus playing tricks.'

Rhianna shook her head vehemently. 'No, it's not Marcus's style,' she told her friend and co-owner of the gallery where they both worked. 'Whatever else my ex-boyfriend might be, I'm sure he's not capable of that sort of behaviour.'

She thought briefly of Marcus and the pain he had caused her when firstly he'd told her he'd found someone else and secondly pulled out of the gallery they'd worked in together. He'd told her their relationship had been going nowhere and, on reflection, she'd known he'd been right. They'd been drifting apart for months.

Fiona scrambled off the stool. 'Forget him,' she advised for the umpteenth time, catching sight of her friend's expression. 'Now, what d'you think of this?'

'It's looking good,' Rhianna said, surveying the effect, head on one side.

The gallery with its white-washed walls was a perfect foil for the vibrant landscape paintings of the local artist.

'Of course there is just one problem . . . '

Fiona glared at her. 'Go on,' she challenged, a glint in her hazel eyes.

'It would be even better if we had any customers.'

Fiona tossed back her mane of red hair. 'Oh, that problem. Well, it's always a bit sluggish this time of year but our online shop is doing well.'

'Huh, the art and craft materials might be flying off the shelves, but we've sold exactly two paintings in the past month.'

'Well, business is always rather slow after Christmas and we're still in a recession. Perhaps we should consider running a few more workshops — now, I could murder a cup of tea. How about you?'

Rhianna nodded. She looked around the small gallery with a sense of pride. Her father had helped her and Fiona to set it up when they'd left art college. It had been the fulfilment of their dreams.

Since her father had died, almost a year ago, they'd made a few changes, but there had always been Marcus in the background, ready to step in should there be any problems. She blinked back the tears.

'Didn't you ever want to know about your family tree?' Fiona asked, as they sat drinking tea and munching digestive biscuits.

'Nope. We were a happy family unit — just the three of us and we had plenty of friends, but now . . . Well, I suppose it would be nice to discover I'd got one or two relatives. I'd always understood I was the last of the Delroy line.'

'Yes, I can't imagine what it must be like to be an only child.'

Rhianna suddenly snapped her fingers. 'I've just remembered something. There was that beautiful floral tribute at Dad's funeral with the message, *Always in my thoughts, M*. I never did discover who'd sent it . . . '

Fiona stared at her. 'And now you're thinking *M* could stand for Mother!'

Rhianna bit her lip. 'Well, it certainly wasn't Marcus. His wreath was very distinctive. Oh, I don't know. It seems a bit far-fetched, doesn't it? I think I'll stick with your theory about someone trying to wind me up.'

They sat in companionable silence, staring out at the bleak February afternoon and the deserted street.

Suddenly Fiona sprang to her feet. 'Great we've got a customer!'

* * *

Rhianna had virtually dismissed the incident when the letter arrived. The woman claiming to be her grandmother had withheld her phone number and Rhianna was the only *Delroy* listed in the directory.

Letitia Delroy's handwriting bore an uncanny resemblance to Rhianna's father, Joe's.

Rhianna read and re-read the letter. It was concise and to the point. Mrs Delroy was very keen to set up a meeting.

'*I could arrange for Mrs Blackett, at the post office, to put you up for a day or two. I enclose her phone number. I've told her to expect a call from a young woman called Rhianna Soames, who was the daughter of a friend of mine. I think it would make sense to keep the real reason for your visit between ourselves for the time being, don't you?*'

Perhaps you could bring some identity with you. Your birth certificate would be good and a photograph of your parents. Also, if you happen to have come across a painting entitled, The Woman in Blue, amongst your father's possessions, I would dearly like a photograph of that.'

'More and more curious,' Fiona said, studying the letter. 'Of course, that's what it's all about, isn't it — this painting. Have you the remotest idea what she's talking about?'

Rhianna frowned. 'Well, yes actually. There is a picture fitting that description in the attic, but I'm sure it isn't worth anything — Dad would have said, wouldn't he? The frame might be worth a few pounds though.'

Fiona handed back the letter. 'Well, there's nothing to stop you going down to that place — wherever it is — is there? I mean the gallery's so quiet at the moment it could practically run itself and we've already discussed closing for a month or two and just running the business online. Why don't you suss it out — otherwise, you'll always be wondering what it's all about.'

Rhianna got cold feet for a moment. 'Will you come with me, Fi?' she asked.

Fiona shook her head. 'No, Rhia this is your thing, not mine and, besides, one of us needs to keep an eye on things here. Anyway, where exactly does this woman live? What's her address?'

'She hasn't given me one. Just the

one for the post office. It's in a village called Brookhurst in Kent.'

'Sounds like a set-up to me. You have to admit it's weird. Would you like me to look this place up on the internet?'

'Yes, please, Fi, that would be brilliant. Somehow, I just can't bring myself to do it.'

Rhianna slipped out to the post office. When she came back, it was to discover there was a customer in the gallery. She registered two things about him; first that he was extremely good-looking, probably mid-thirties, with a mop of rich chestnut hair and a finely chiselled profile and, second, that he was looking intently at their computer.

'Hello, can I help you?' she asked coolly.

Startled, he looked up and she found herself gazing into a pair of eyes that were like chips of jade. She swallowed, finding his intense stare unnerving.

'Sorry. I'm afraid I'm something of a computer bod. It's my line of business along with dabbling in painting, as I was explaining to your colleague just now.'

'I see — well please feel free to take a look around. Is there something in particular we can help you with?'

'Oh, actually, I was just passing and thought I'd take a look — never could resist a gallery. I love the colours of those paintings. They're very vibrant.'

'Yes, that's a collection from a local artist, Matt Collins. He's extremely talented. We try to support as many as we can. Are you a collector?'

He shook his head. 'Regretfully, no. I'm afraid I don't have the space, but I sometimes buy for other people. You don't have any portraits?'

'Not at the moment, no, but we try to change our exhibitions on a regular basis so it's worth dropping by, although we've only just finished assembling this one.'

To Rhianna's relief, Fiona reappeared at that moment, clutching a couple of catalogues and some postcards which she handed to the man.

'So what do you two do? Is any of

your work exhibited here?'

Fiona pointed to her sculptures. 'Those are mine. Rhianna is very versatile — as you can see from the postcards. At present, she just has those photographs of the Queen's Diamond Jubilee at the far end.'

Rhianna pushed back a strand of honey-blonde hair, uncomfortably aware that the man's attention was focussed on her.

'I'm inclined to work from photographs — land and seascapes — mainly watercolours and oils. Sometimes, I do pastel drawings — mostly of animals or children.'

His green eyes were full of interest. 'Very impressive.' He crossed to the display of photographs. 'Wow! These are amazing.'

'And what about you?' she asked curiously.

He was still studying her photographs. 'Oh, as I've said, I try my hand at painting, but it's mainly a hobby.'

Shortly afterwards, the visitor departed.

'Fi, you really ought to be more

careful. He was looking at our computer.'

Fiona raised her eyebrows. 'So where's the harm in that? It's his line of business — computers. He told me so. Drop dead gorgeous, wasn't he?'

Rhianna pursed her lips. 'If you say so. Can't say I noticed.'

Fiona laughed. 'You're a hopeless case, don't you know that? How could you have helped noticing that physique? He must have been at least six foot tall and in really good shape. Bet he works out.'

Rhianna shrugged. 'I'm not the slightest bit interested. Have a heart, Fi! I'm just getting over one broken relationship and — so far as I'm concerned — men are a lost cause . . . Anyway, whatever would Dave say?'

Fiona grinned as she thought about her current boyfriend.

'Oh, Dave's not the jealous type. Besides, he knows we're solid. Now, let's have a brain-storming session to see if we can come up with some

brilliant ideas for some more workshops.'

★   ★   ★

Letitia Delroy picked up the phone and
listened intently as Lawrence told her
about his recent trip to the gallery.

'So, what conclusion did you come
to, Laurie?'

'She'll do,' he told her. 'You'll like
her.'

He had no intention of telling Letitia
of the impact Rhianna had made on
him. He had a sudden vision of her
slim, well-proportioned figure, hair like
spun gold and expressive, deep-blue
eyes — like sapphires, he'd decided.

Letitia let out a sigh of relief. 'And
what's this gallery like?'

'I've told you, Tish. It's in a cottage
in the high street — two rooms knocked
into one. Quite small, but adequate.
Both girls have an eye for display and
their website is pretty good too.'

Letitia smoothed her white hair

13

nervously. 'And did you, er, see any sign of the portrait?'

'I'm afraid not. There were no portraits there at all — just some rather colourful landscapes by a local artist and a few animal sculptures, oh and some superb local photographs that Rhianna had taken of the Queen's Diamond Jubilee celebrations.'

'Well, perhaps Joe sold it. You didn't ask?'

He laughed. 'No, Tish, I didn't ask. How could I, without explaining my real purpose for being there? You'll just have to be patient.'

'Do you think she'll come to see me?' Letitia asked now.

'Look, don't get your hopes up,' he told her. 'I've sussed things out like you've asked me to. Rhianna Delroy is a young woman who knows her own mind. I could tell that from our very brief acquaintance. Other than that, I can't say. We're just going to have to wait and see.'

Letitia sighed. 'Well, thank you for

everything, Laurie. It would be wonderful if she came.'

'Yes, I hope she does,' Lawrence told
her sincerely. 'Look, keep me informed.
Let me know what's happening, won't
you? If she does decide to visit you,
then I'll make a point of being there
too. I'd like to see what transpires.'

And he'd like to get to know Rhianna
Delroy better. He had had his own
reasons for that.

★ ★ ★

Fiona rang Rhianna that evening. 'Rhia
I've looked up the Brookhurst Post
Office. It's all perfectly bona fide. You've
nothing to worry about in that respect.
And, listen to this. I've also had a go at
looking up *Delroy*. It seems that your
grandfather *was* born in Kent. Reginald
Delroy married a Letitia Horton and
they had one son, Joseph, who must
have been your father.

'Spooky, isn't it, to find you've got a
grandmother after all this time when

15

you thought she was dead — it's like a voice from the grave! Exciting though!'

That wasn't the word Rhianna would have used for it. She felt a little shiver run down her spine. What was she going to do now? She had two options — to ignore the situation or suss it out. If she did nothing it would always be at the back of her mind and, one day, she would wish she'd done something about it.

On an impulse, she decided to ring Mrs Blackett the following morning. She seemed to be a perfectly normal lady who had been expecting Rhianna's call.

'I'll look forward to seeing you on Thursday,' she told her.

Rhianna could only hope she wasn't making the biggest mistake of her life.

* * *

It was a slow journey to Brookhurst because several of the roads were poorly signposted. The twisting lanes were so narrow that there was no room to manoeuvre. She was stuck behind a tractor for what seemed like an eternity.

The only reason she could come up with for making this madcap journey was curiosity and an overriding desire to get away for a while and shake off all remaining memories of Marcus.

As Fiona had said, it was time to move on. Rhianna intended to recharge her batteries, and throw herself into the business; there would definitely be no place for men in her life from now on!

A couple of times she lost her way and had to double back along lanes no wider than tracks. The shadows were lengthening. Just as she was beginning to think she would never find the village, she went through a wooded area and suddenly, over the rise of a hill, she spotted some ragstone houses nestling down below and smoke spiralling into the grey sky. Signs of habitation at last!

A van suddenly shot out of a side turning and hurtled towards her. She swerved, narrowly avoiding it. Shaken, she saw the sign post read, *Brookhurst 2 miles*. The natives round here aren't very friendly, she decided. She heaved a sigh of relief when she finally reached Brookhurst. She parked near to the post office and, walking back the short distance rattled the handle. The sign read *OPEN* — but it was shut. She frowned. It was only about four thirty. Now what? A woman crossed the road towards her.

'Is she closed? That's odd; I was in there a little while ago. My daughter-in-law works in the shop.'

'I'm supposed to be staying with Mrs Blackett,' Rhianna told her.

'Oh, yes you've come to see Mrs Delroy, haven't you? I'm Irene Blake, by the way.'

Irene peered through the post office window. 'Oh dear Lord! I think that's Mavis lying on the floor. Quick! Let's see if we can get in round the back.'

Filled with a dreadful premonition, Rhianna followed Irene along a narrow passageway that led to the back of the shop. Her suspicions were confirmed. The gate was hanging off its hinges and the back door was open.

A muffled sound, accompanied by a bumping noise, came from the kitchen. Lizzie was tied to a chair, a scarf bound tightly round her mouth.

'Lizzie. Oh, my dear girl what have they done to you?'

Rhianna went to the aid of Mavis Blackett who was lying half behind the counter. She bent over her, trying to remember her first aid.

'Mrs Blackett's unconscious — think she's been hit over the head,' she called out and, whipping out her mobile, phoned for the police and an ambulance.

Much later, after the ambulance had taken Mavis Blackett and Lizzie to the hospital with a policeman and Irene Blake following behind, Rhianna gratefully accepted the cup of tea offered her by the remaining policewoman.

'So tell me about this white van you saw at the crossroads. Take your time.'

Rhianna explained all over again what happened.

'I'm supposed to be staying here tonight,' she said anxiously. 'It's getting a bit late to go home now. Besides, I've arranged to see Mrs Delroy. She's elderly so I can't expect her to accommodate me.'

'Well, let's see if the proprietor of the *White Unicorn* can put you up.'

As Rhianna followed the policewoman into the bar of the pub, she was uncomfortably aware that all eyes were turned on her as everyone waited to hear what had happened. Fortunately, the policewoman explained briefly adding, 'this young lady had arranged to stay with Mrs Blackett but, of course, that's out of the question now. Is it possible for you to put her up?'

Was it her imagination or did the proprietor's expression change when the policewoman mentioned Mrs Delroy?

He ran his fingers through his thinning hair. 'Well, I'd best have a word with the missus. We don't usually have guests during the winter months, but I reckon we could make an exception in the circumstances.'

'Friend of Mrs Delroy's, are you Miss?' enquired a portly, red-faced man sitting on a bar stool.

'No, my parents were. Actually we've never met.'

'I see — well, I expect she'll be glad of a bit of company. She's rather housebound these days. Doesn't get out much at all.' He turned to the police woman. 'Wasn't there an incident up at *Wisteria Lodge*, last week?'

'There was a bit of a problem, yes, but I'm not at liberty to divulge any details.'

Rhianna wondered what exactly she'd got herself into. Brookhurst wasn't turning out to be quite the idyllic, peaceful spot she'd imagined. She'd stay the one night, visit Mrs Blackett at the hospital and see Letitia Delroy as arranged and then consider going home.

'I think I'll pay Mrs Delroy a visit whilst I'm in the area. Want to come with me?' the policewoman asked Rhianna.

'Oh, I — um — actually, I think it might be best if I left it until tomorrow morning.'

The policewoman nodded. 'Well, we can at least speak with her on the phone.'

'Sorry, I'm afraid I don't have her number. She didn't give it to me — only Mrs Blackett's.'

She received some strange glances and supposed it did sound odd.

The proprietor found the number and everyone listened as the police-woman explained briefly what had happened.

'Now, I'm coming up to see you in a few minutes, Mrs Delroy. I've got a young lady here who's called Rhianna Soames — says you're expecting her. You are? That's fine.' She passed the phone to Rhianna.

'Hello, Mrs Delroy, it's Rhianna. I'm absolutely fine, thank you. I'm going to be staying at the *White Unicorn*. How about I come to see you tomorrow morning around eleven thirty?'

Once the policewoman had gone, Rhianna found herself the centre of attention. 'So tell us your version of events,' the man on the bar stool invited. 'It sounded pretty nasty to me. Was she coshed over the 'ead?'

Rhianna decided not to go into details. 'She did have a head wound, yes. Anyway, she's in safe hands now and Lizzie Blake has got her mother-in-law with her, so everything's been taken care of.'

Presently, when Rhianna moved her car into the pub car park she discovered there was a police cordon outside the post office.

'Crime scene now,' Ron the proprietor said dourly. 'Nothing much happens here and then we get two incidents in the space of a week.'

'We're not safe in our beds no more,' the man on the bar stool commented cryptically looking up from his beer.

Ron handed Rhianna a drink. 'Here

get that down you, lass. You look as if you could do with it. It's on the house. Unfortunate introduction to your stay in Brookhurst. Hope the experience won't put you off. Don't know what the world's coming to!'

2

Ron's wife, Iris, appeared shortly afterwards and showed Rhianna to her room. It was very basic accommodation but spotlessly clean and besides, beggars couldn't be choosers, Rhianna reflected. She unpacked her few belongings, had a wash and brush-up and, feeling peckish, went in search of food.

To her disappointment, all she was offered was a bowl of soup and some sandwiches with a small side salad. It seemed hot meals were off the agenda. After sending a text to Fiona, she decided to have an early night.

She didn't expect to sleep and was thankful for the book she'd brought with her, even though it was a murder mystery! She found herself listening to every little sound. Her head was buzzing with the day's events. Something had made her tell everyone her name was Rhianna

Soames and she could have sworn there had been one or two looks exchanged. She supposed it had been a mistake to give a false name to the police!

★   ★   ★

In the cold light of day, Rhianna reluctantly got out of bed and, grabbing her dressing-gown and wash-bag, padded along to the bathroom which was adequate but hardly luxurious. She was towelling herself down after her shower when the door handle rattled impatiently. She hurriedly finished off and, scooping up her things, opened the door to practically canon into someone.

The man standing there — tall, broad-shouldered and naked to the waist — looked vaguely familiar and then their eyes met and she gasped as she met the cool-green gaze of the man from the gallery.

He raised his eyebrows. 'Sorree, I didn't realise anyone else was staying here.'

'That makes two of us,' she grunted,

wondering if he'd recognised her. His eyes swept over her and she instinctively pulled her robe more closely about her, unable to avoid noticing his firm skin and rippling muscles.

'Haven't we met before?' he asked suddenly.

'You came into my gallery last week,' she told him. It would be senseless to deny it.

'Oh, of course. Forgive me — but well, what a coincidence!'

'But was it?' she asked herself, as she hurried back to her room. A slight shiver ran through her. Had he followed her to Brookhurst and if so what could possibly be his motive?

★ ★ ★

Lawrence whistled to himself in the shower. He was naturally sorry about the post office raid but it was amazing to think that, as a result, Rhianna Delroy was now staying under the same roof as him. That had to be providential. He

27

thought of the trim shape revealed by the figure-hugging dressing-gown, remembered the fleeting moment when she had brushed her arm against his. He'd caught a slight waft of some flowery fragrance, felt the softness of her skin.

Whatever was he thinking of? Women were off the agenda as far as he was concerned. They caused far too many complications and he was certain that this one would be no exception.

*   *   *

Rhianna hurriedly got dressed and applied a modicum of make-up. Her mind was on overdrive. This was extremely weird. It couldn't be a coincidence that the visitor from their gallery had turned up here. She didn't know what game he was playing, but she was determined to find out.

She hurried downstairs and hesitated, wondering where breakfast would be served. As she entered the bar, the man she'd just been thinking about looked up, immaculate now in a spot-less white shirt and dark jeans, a sweater draped casually round his shoulders. She found it hard to believe that he was already sitting there, halfway through eating a bowl of cereal.

She sat herself at an adjacent table and studied the breakfast menu Ron bought her.

'So what brings you to this neck of the woods?' her breakfast companion asked conversationally.

She said the first thing that entered her head. 'Oh, it was a favourite haunt of my late father's. Call it a nostalgia trip, if you like. I'm going to be visiting an old friend of his.'

'Nothing to do with art then?' he asked casually.

She shook her head. 'Not on this occasion — what about you?'

'Oh, I'm having a bit of a busman's holiday. I've promised to update Ron's website and I'm also looking at property in the area, with a view to settling here.

'I lived here a while back for a short

time and like the place. It holds a certain attraction for me — rural but not too far from civilisation. Great place for painting too.'

Personally, Rhianna thought February was a strange time to come and visit, but perhaps he was doing Ron a favour. He picked up his newspaper and that seemed a signal that the conversation was ended. She ate a leisurely breakfast and was pouring a second cup of coffee when he got to his feet.

'We haven't introduced ourselves,' he said extending a hand, 'which seems odd when we're sharing a bathroom.'

A slight colour tinged her cheeks, as she had an image of his naked torso, and she lowered her eyes away from his amused gaze. It was as if he could read her thoughts!

'I'm Lawrence Lorimer — Laurie to my friends.'

'Well, I'm sure you know who I am.' She hesitated, not sure whether to introduce herself as *Soames* or *Delroy*. In the end she just said, 'I'm Rhianna, but my friends call me Rhia.'

He gave her a devastating smile. 'Please to meet you, Rhia.'

★ ★ ★

Rhianna bought some flowers at a garage on the way to the hospital, which was quite a drive away. When she arrived, she realised that she'd had a fruitless journey.

'I'm afraid Mrs Blackett's not up to receiving visitors at the moment,' the young nurse told her. 'Besides, the police are still waiting to question her when she's well enough.'

She took the flowers from Rhianna.

'I'll see that she gets these. Who shall I say they're from?'

'Rhianna Soames.'

The nurse looked startled. 'Well, it was your name she spoke when she first came round. You must have been on her mind.'

When Rhianna got back to the hospital car park, she encountered

Irene Blake and Lizzie.

'Oh, I'm so glad we've run into you. Lizzie and I wanted to thank you for all you did yesterday. Didn't we, Lizzie?'

Lizzie, who looked pale, but otherwise unscathed, nodded.

'They've discharged me but Mavis is still very poorly. It's a funny thing but before she was hit over the 'ead that criminal was asking after you.'

'Me — ' Rhianna exclaimed horrified. 'Are you sure?'

Lizzie nodded. 'He definitely said he wanted to speak to the *Soames* woman — wouldn't believe Mavis when she told him you hadn't arrived.'

A cold chill filled her. Whoever could have known she would be here? And then she thought of Lawrence Lorimer!

'We thought we ought to warn you dear, just in case — perhaps you should tell the police,' Irene added.

'Oh, I intend to,' she assured them and hurried off to her car. Her mobile trilled and she snatched it from her bag. It was Fiona.

'Rhianna! Thank God! I've been so worried. Are you OK? I was at a concert with Dave last night and didn't pick up your message until this morning. I've only just heard the news about the post office raid. I've been imagining all sorts of things.'

'Fiona, if you would just let me get a word in edgeways! I'm absolutely fine, just a bit shaken. I got lost on the way down and it all happened just before I arrived.'

'I thought you might be dead!' Fiona wailed dramatically.

'No, I'm alive and kicking, although poor Mrs Blackett is still in hospital. It's all very weird, Fiona.'

'You can say that again. So where are you staying? Are you coming home soon?'

'At the pub, and no, not for the moment.'

'Have you spoken with the woman claiming to be your grandmother yet?'

'No, I'm going up there presently. At the moment I'm at the hospital. They wouldn't let me see Mrs Blackett. She's too poorly. The police are waiting to interview her.'

Rhianna told her friend what Lizzie had said.

'That's decidedly spooky. They must have got it wrong. Why would anyone be looking for you? I mean, who even knows you're there? Oh, there's a customer. Quick! Tell me the name of the pub where you're staying.'

'The *White Unicorn* — ask for Rhianna *Soames*. Come to think of it I've given a false name to a policeman!'

'You've what?' shrieked Fiona.

'And Fiona, listen, I haven't told you the oddest bit yet. That chap who came into the gallery — the tall, good-looking one. He's turned up here. I keep thinking he must have known I was coming here, although I can't figure out how . . . Fi, are you still there?'

But Fiona had rung off and Rhianna just hoped she'd caught the name of the pub where she was staying.

By the time Rhianna got back to

Brookhurst, it was still only ten forty five. She had an inspiration. She'd take a look at the church which she'd discovered was just outside the village, near a picturesque duck pond and a large green. It was within easy walking distance.

The door was unlocked and creaked protestingly as she entered. There was no-one about and she spent a few minutes wandering about. It was fairly dark inside, apart from the wintry sunlight which filtered through the stained glass windows making dancing rainbow patterns on the floor.

She discovered a couple of brass memorial plates set in the stone wall near the altar, bearing the name of *Delroy*. She gazed at them in fascination, wondering if they really could be her ancestors.

Suddenly she heard footsteps behind her. Whirling round she saw a middle-aged man coming towards her in clerical robes. He smiled.

'Hello, sorry, I didn't mean to alarm

you. I'm the vicar, here. We don't get many visitors this time of year. Were you wanting to do some brass rubbing?'

She took a deep breath. 'Actually, no. I'm staying at the pub — supposed to be meeting up with Letitia Delroy shortly.'

He looked surprised. 'Oh, that's nice. She doesn't have many visitors.' He stretched out his hand, 'Tim Holt.'

'Rhianna Soames.'

His eyes widened. 'Did you say *Soames?*' There was a strange expression on his face but then he smiled. 'Welcome to St Peters'. Look, this is the one place where I can actually invite you to take a pew! Are you related to Christina?'

She shook her head and sat down beside him.

'Christina?' she echoed, puzzled. Who on earth was Christina, she wondered. 'Not as far as I'm aware. So were the *Delroys* an influential family round here?'

'Once, a long time ago, they were significant land-owners, I believe, but now there's only Reg Delroy's widow.'

'Actually,' she told him, making up her mind suddenly to come clean, 'that's my real purpose for being here. My real name is Rhianna *Delroy*. I've come to find out if I'm Letitia Delroy's granddaughter.'

Tim Holt stroked his chin thoughtfully. As a vicar he thought he'd heard everything, but this was a complete surprise. His kindly brown eyes gave nothing away. The girl seemed genuine enough.

'Indeed. Tell you what, why don't I make us both a coffee? You look as if you could do with one and then you can tell me all about it. We've a small kitchenette through there and can even run to a filter.'

'I'd like that — except I've arranged to see Letitia Delroy at eleven thirty.'

'Oh, it won't matter if you're a bit late, my wife's with her at the moment. She pops in from time to time. Tell you what, I'll give her a ring, tell her you're with me.'

Over coffee and ginger cookies she

told Tim briefly what she was doing in Brookhurst. After all, surely she could trust a vicar and a church seemed the appropriate place for confessions and sanctuary.

'Well, that's quite a story,' Tim said when she'd finished. 'It's just unfortunate Letitia saw fit to ask you to use the name *Soames*.'

'Why?' she asked, puzzled.

For answer he took her by the arm and led her out of a side door into the churchyard. They paused before a family grave and she read the inscriptions on the headstone.

'They're all Soames — Elizabeth, Derek and their daughter Anna!' she mused. 'So who were they?'

'Elizabeth Soames, or Betty as everyone called her, was a great friend of Letitia's. Anna was her daughter. As you can see, Betty outlived both her husband and her daughter.

'Now, I have to say that I only know what I've gleaned from those who knew Anna, but I gather she was a bewitching young woman who was rather free with her favours. She fell pregnant and sadly died in childbirth. Betty and her husband brought up the child, Christina.

'After her husband died Betty struggled on alone, but it wasn't easy. Tina was a difficult girl.'

'What about the father?' Rhianna asked, intrigued.

Tim hesitated and then cleared his throat. 'There's always been speculation but, to this day, no-one really seems to know who the father was. Betty did her best for the child, but her health wasn't good and when Tina was in her teens, Betty had a stroke and died too.

'From then on Letitia acted as a guardian to Christina, treated her as a member of her own family. It seems it was something Betty had asked her to do.'

'So that's why you asked if I knew Christina. Where is she now?'

Tim sighed. 'Letitia financed her through university, but she got in with a wild crowd and, the moment she'd finished, went off abroad. After a while, she came back here and seemed to settle down — found herself a job and a decent boyfriend, got engaged and we all thought things were looking up.'

He paused and then continued. 'Unfortunately, she met up again with some of her former friends. They were a bad influence on her. This time, Letitia refused to bale her out. Tina, as everyone calls her, said she was going to France *to find herself*, as she put it, whatever that meant. But then a few months ago she came back again and told Letitia she needed to go to Australia but she hadn't any money, as usual.'

'So I suppose Mrs Delroy gave it to her?'

Tim sighed. 'You suppose right. Letitia very foolishly put her hand in her pocket again and Tina took off. We haven't heard a word from her since.'

Rhianna tried to get her head round all this. 'I still don't understand why Letitia asked me to call myself Rhianna *Soames*.'

'I would think it's just so she could identify you — like a password — if you see what I mean. Perhaps she wasn't thinking straight . . . Now, I've arranged to pick up my wife from *Wisteria Lodge*, so how about leaving the car here and coming with me? I can collect you later. It might make the situation easier for the pair of you.'

Rhianna felt increasingly nervous as she approached *Wisteria Lodge*. Supposing it had all been an elaborate hoax — part of the post office raid and, somehow, she'd been implicated? She moistened her lips. What if Mrs Delroy didn't back up her story? She had used a false name. Perhaps she could end up in a police cell.

But Rhianna need not have worried. The door was flung open by a still attractive woman in her sixties.

'Myra, this is Rhianna. She's come to see Letitia.'

Myra Holt's face creased into a smile. 'Come along in, my dear, she's expecting you.'

The moment Rhianna walked into the sitting-room she knew, without a shadow of doubt, that the elderly, frail little woman in the armchair by the fire was her grandmother. She was the spitting image of her father.

A surge of emotions hit Rhianna so that, for a moment, she was frozen to the spot. Myra gave her a gentle push.

'Rhianna oh Rhianna you came!'

'I'll make some coffee,' Myra said tactfully. 'Come along Tim, you can help me.'

And they were left alone.

There was a long pause and then Letitia asked softly, 'Did you bring the things I asked about?'

For an answer, Rhianna delved into her handbag and produced her birth certificate.

'And here is a photograph of my parents and one of the painting you were asking about.'

She passed them across to Letitia who studied them in silence for what seemed like eternity. Eventually, she looked up and nodded.

'If I had any doubts left in my mind they would be dispelled by now. That is definitely my son, Joseph Delroy, and you, my dear; you take after your father. You've got his eyes.'

Letitia looked long and hard at the photograph of the painting of *The Woman in Blue*. 'So your father didn't get rid of it,' she murmured.

'What is it with that painting?' Rhianna asked. 'Have you any idea who it is?'

Letitia nodded. 'It's Anna Soames, of course.'

Rhianna stared at her. 'But until I came here, I'd never even heard of Anna Soames. What is the connection . . . ?' she began mystified.

'Didn't your father ever mention her to you?'

Rhianna shook her head. 'No, but this morning, before I came up here, Tim Holt told me a little and he showed me the graves. He also mentioned Christina.'

'Ah, yes, Christina.' Letitia suddenly looked upset. 'Christina was Anna's daughter. She's gone to Australia.'

'I see. Mrs Delroy, I need to ask you, why have you chosen to get in touch now? After all this time?'

Letitia looked at her sadly. 'Couldn't you bring yourself to call me, *Grandmother?*'

Rhianna swallowed. 'It's all so strange. It's going to take time. Until a short time ago, I thought I was the end of the Delroy line.'

Letitia reached out and patted her arm. 'I understand, dear. Then couldn't you call me Letitia for the time being?'

Rhianna nodded. It was a compromise. She was beginning to warm to this elderly lady.

Myra came back just then with a tray of coffee and biscuits and a promise to return for Rhianna in an hour or so.

After they'd gone, Rhianna said tentatively, 'Yesterday someone said there'd been an incident here.'

Letitia Delroy nodded. 'There was a prowler — lights in the grounds, things moved about in the summer house and worse than that.'

The elderly lady looked distressed.

Rhianna moved closer to her. 'What happened?' she prompted gently.

'Someone let off fireworks. It frightened poor Tansy.'

'Tansy?' Rhianna asked, mystified.

'My little West-Highland terrier.'

As if on cue, Tansy, who'd apparently been asleep behind the sofa all this time, suddenly put in an appearance wagging her tail.

'Probably just some youths being silly,' Rhianna told her, patting the little dog. It certainly wasn't much to go on.

Letitia nodded. 'That's what the police said, but I can't help thinking there's more to it than that. You see the other day, there was a dead crow in the porch.'

Rhianna looked blank. 'I'm sorry, I'm not sure I see the significance.'

'Tim would be annoyed with me for saying this but, in these parts, a crow can be a portent of misfortune.'

Rhianna was trying to make some

sense of this, but was finding it difficult.

'Oh, dear, you're going to think I'm just a foolish old woman, but since Tina left, I'm afraid I've become quite jittery.'

'Have you heard from Tina since she went to Australia?'

Letitia shook her head. 'No, just a very quick phone call to say she'd arrived.'

There was a sudden loud rap on the door. Rhianna answered it to find two policemen standing on the step. One was the officer who had interviewed her the previous day.

'Rhianna Soames. I need to ask you a few questions.'

Rhianna smiled at him. 'Fire away but I should tell you I'm not Rhianna Soames. I'm Rhianna *Delroy*.'

He stared at her frowningly. 'But yesterday you said — you definitely told me you were Rhianna *Soames*.'

'Yes, I know and I'm sorry.'

She led the way into the sitting-room and produced her birth-certificate again.

'So, why on earth did you give me the name *Soames?*'

Letitia came to her rescue. 'Oh, it was just a name I asked Rhianna to use. I needed to be sure, you see, that she really was my granddaughter. It was like a password.'

The policeman looked unconvinced and Rhianna whipped a business card out of her bag.

'You can look me up on the website if you like or ring the gallery. My friend, Fiona Field, will vouch for me.'

'You're an artist?'

She nodded, relieved that she seemed to be getting through to him at last. 'Yes, our gallery's at this address in Hertfordshire. That's how Mrs Delroy tracked me down.'

He scratched his chin and said, 'I don't know what to make of all this. If you're not Rhianna Soames then why did Mrs Blackett say you were?'

Letitia smiled. 'That's easy, I booked her in in that name — saved speculation and it seemed best until we got to know each other, but now, after what's happened . . . I'm not so sure.'

'I've been told those men were asking for me by name at the post office,' Rhianna said worriedly, and shuddered.

The policeman rubbed his ear. 'Yes, well, giving yourself a false name probably wasn't the wisest thing to do in the circumstances. It seems those criminals might have thought you were someone else . . . Now, are you going to be around for the next few days, Miss — er — Delroy? We may need to question you again.'

Rhianna nodded. 'Yes, I can be contacted at the *White Unicorn* if you need me.'

'Or here. You'll be spending some time with me, won't you, dear?' Letitia said quietly.

Rhianna nodded. Suddenly everything seemed surreal. How had she come to be in this situation with an elderly woman who claimed to be her grandmother? Had she made a dreadful mistake in coming here? But, she was

sure there was a distinct family resemblance and, suddenly, she really wanted
to believe that Letitia Delroy was her
grandmother.

3

'So, how did you track me down?' Rhianna asked Letitia, after the police had gone.

'I found your business card along with some cuttings about the gallery in a drawer in Tina's room, after she'd left. To be honest, it gave me quite a shock. I knew your father had died — I saw the obituary in *The Telegraph* which is how I found out about your existence.'

'But why would Tina have my card?'

Letitia shook her head. 'I've been trying to puzzle that out and I don't have an answer.'

A feeling of unease shot through Rhianna.

Seeing her expression Letitia said, 'Perhaps Tina was worried about me being on my own. I used to have a cousin but she died last year. We were never a big family.'

'So what happened?' Rhianna asked. 'I mean how come my father cut himself off from you?'

For a long moment Letitia didn't reply and then she said in a quiet voice, 'Sometimes in this life we have to make choices. Mine was between my husband and my son. In the end I chose Reg. It was the hardest decision I ever made.

'Joe took off and I never set eyes on him again. As I've said, I didn't even know you existed until I read the obituary.'

It was obvious Letitia wasn't prepared to say anything more and shortly afterwards Tim Holt arrived to pick Rhianna up.

'Myra's invited you to supper,' he told her during the short drive back to the village. 'They're not doing hot meals at the pub until the kitchen's refurbished. I'd love to know how you got on, but I'm due at a meeting shortly so you'll have to keep me in suspense until this evening.'

'Thanks — that would be brilliant,' Rhianna told him gratefully.

As Tim parked at the side of the *White Unicorn*, she saw Lawrence Lorimer just getting out of his car.

'Wow! There's a blast from the past!' Tim exclaimed.

'Do you know him?' Rhianna asked in relieved surprise.

'Absolutely. Lawrence used to live in Brookhurst — obviously, Letitia hasn't said anything.'

'About what?' But Tim did not reply. He wound down the window.

'Laurie — long time no see!' he called out and Lawrence raised his hand in greeting and came across to the car.

Thanking Tim again, Rhianna slipped away and hurried into the pub. Going upstairs, she stopped to look out of a side window on the landing. She could see Lawrence still in conversation with Tim. She was curious to know what it was Letitia hadn't said.

Rhianna wondered what she would find to do that afternoon. She'd brought her sketch book, but it was too chilly to stand about and so she decided to take some photographs. She could work from those at home and make a record of the village where her father had been brought up.

Collecting up her camera, she went downstairs again. She could have done with some lunch but didn't want to run into Lawrence Lorimer. When she went into the bar there was no sign of him, however, and Lizzie and Irene Blake were tucking into a ploughman's in the far corner.

'Come and join us,' they invited when they saw her hesitating.

She ordered a toasted sandwich and orange juice and took her drink across to their table.

'Lizzie's feeling a bit lost today, as the post office is still closed, so I've brought her in here to cheer her up. Did you get to see Mrs Delroy?'

'Yes, we had a long chat. I met the vicar when I went in the church and he ran me up there. He's invited me to supper tonight.'

'That's nice. We're quite a friendly

bunch in this village really.'

'Did you — er — happen to know Tina Soames?' she asked casually.

Lizzie and her Irene exchanged glances. 'Yes, we knew Tina,' Lizzie said. 'Wait a minute, your name's *Soames*, isn't it? Are you related to her?'

'Oh, no, not so far as I'm aware,' Rhianna said. 'I understand Mrs Delroy brought her up when her grandmother died.'

'Mmm, and that young woman gave her a really hard time. Gone to Australia now, so they say, and good riddance to her.'

Before Rhianna could ask her what she meant, Ron brought her sandwich and stopped to chat, mainly about the post office raid. When he'd gone Lizzie said, 'You know, I've been thinking. I wouldn't be surprised if that criminal yesterday thought it was Tina Soames who was staying at the post office. I mean — why would he be after you?'

Rhianna pulled a wry face. 'That's what I've been trying to work out. I haven't got the remotest idea.'

This had confirmed her suspicions. It seemed far more plausible that the raiders were looking for Tina. It was an obvious case of mistaken identity, but how had they known someone by the name of *Soames* would be staying with Mavis Blackett? She kept coming back to Lawrence. She felt uncomfortable and wished Marcus was around so that she could talk it through with him.

Irene and Lizzie drew Rhianna a little map of the village and told her some of the best places to visit.

'You might find some snowdrops if you go along that path at the back of the village hall. Well, I suppose we'd best be going now. Nice to have seen you again.'

★ ★ ★

Rhianna had a productive afternoon. The countryside, although rather bleak at this time of year, was still worth photographing.

She took the path Irene had suggested and came across a mass of snowdrops, together with quantities of golden aconites nestling beneath a chestnut tree in a cottage garden. She could see for miles across the fields where sheep were grazing. It was a tranquil scene.

Presently, she found the school and wondered if her father had attended it when he was a child. She realised she knew virtually nothing about his childhood. She became so engrossed in what she was doing that the time flew by. She was pleased with her afternoon's work. When she next saw Letitia, as she still thought of her grandmother, she would ask her about the places in the locality her father had visited.

Returning to the *White Unicorn*, she soaked in a leisurely bath. She hadn't brought many clothes with her and wondered what would be suitable attire for dinner at the vicarage. In the end, she teamed a pair of black trousers with a peacock-blue embroidered top and, thinking it might be chilly, grabbed a jacket.

As she walked along the corridor towards the stairs, a floorboard squeaked behind her and a hand touched her shoulder. Stifling a scream, she span round to find Lawrence Lorimer standing there.

'Rhia I'm so sorry, I didn't mean to alarm you.'

Rhianna was trembling and catching her arms, he pulled her to him and held her for a moment. 'It's OK, Rhianna, I'm not going to hurt you,' he assured her.

Her heart was thumping wildly. She was aware of the warmth of his body against hers, the gleam of his green eyes — the fresh woody scent of his cologne.

'Wh-what do you want?' she almost whispered.

'Only to tell you that I've been invited to the vicarage tonight too and thought we could both go in my car.'

'Oh.' He felt her relax against him and gently took her hand.

'How did you know where I was?' she asked, aware of his fingers encircling her wrist, comforting and firm.

'I saw you walking along the corridor.'

'No — I mean how did you know I was in Brookhurst? You came here because of me, didn't you?'

There was a small scar on his cheek and she wondered how he'd come by it. His green eyes sparked and she moved away.

'Yes, but I didn't follow you, as you seem to imagine, nor did I have anything to do with the raid.'

'So why are you here?'

He hesitated. 'I'd rather not discuss it standing in a corridor. Even the walls seem to have ears in this place. Rhianna you need to trust me.'

Her dark-blue eyes gave him a penetrating gaze. 'Give me one good reason why I should?'

'Will you at least listen to me — give me a chance to explain before someone else does?'

She sighed. 'Oh, very well.'

He led her back along the corridor to his room.

Reluctantly, she followed him inside and sat on the armchair. He perched on the edge of the bed.

'Letitia is one of the nicest people I know, generous and kind, but she is also gullible and, so when she told me about you, I was naturally concerned for her and offered to see if I could find out whether you really were her granddaughter.'

'So you came to the gallery to check me out. But, why? What is Letitia to you?' she asked curiously.

'I'm very fond of Letitia. At one time, I was practically a part of her family and I'm still very protective of her. Even though I haven't been around for the past couple of years, I've always kept in touch.'

'What do you mean, 'you were part of her family?'' Rhianna asked, puzzled.

'Have you heard of Christina Soames?'

She frowned. 'Not until this morning but, since then, that name has cropped up a number of times. So what is the connection between you and Christina?'

There was a pause during which Lawrence laced and unlaced his fingers and then he said, 'For a short time she was my fiancée.'

Rhianna stared at him as things slowly began to slot into place.

'Right — now I'm beginning to understand. So do you know where she is? Because it seems as if she's the person those criminals were looking for yesterday and not me.'

Lawrence sighed. 'Yes, I realise that and I'm sorry you got involved, although I can assure you, I have absolutely no idea how this could have happened. It truly wasn't down to me. I'm not in touch with Tina now, but she did have a number of dubious friends.'

'Letitia thinks she's gone to Australia.'

He shrugged. 'Who's to say? She could be absolutely anywhere. The world's a big place.'

He caught her hands in his. 'Do you think we could begin again and be friends? After all, we both have the interests of Letitia at heart, don't we?'

She nodded. 'That'd be great. It's better than being enemies.'

She gave a slight smile and he pulled her to her feet. Leaning forward he touched her gently on the cheek and her pulse raced.

'We'll get through this together,' he told her softly.

A little shaft of fear shot through her.

'Get through what? What do you mean?'

'Oh, absolutely nothing — just a figure of speech,' he assured her, but she was not convinced.

Lawrence picked up his car keys. 'Now, if we don't want to be late for that meal, we'd best get a move on.'

'I should have got something for Myra and Tim,' she said, as she followed him downstairs.

'Well, that's easily solved,' he stopped at the bar and purchased a couple of bottles of wine. She made to pay him but he waved her money aside.

'My shout. Accept it as an apology for alarming you just now. Now, we can look forward to a good evening. Tim and Myra are excellent company and Myra's cooking is legendary.

'Before I forget, I was speaking to Letitia earlier. She's invited both of us to lunch tomorrow. I've got to work in the morning but that gives you a chance to spend some quality time with her.

★   ★   ★

The Vicarage was rambling and rather shabby. Myra had cooked a huge meal, roast chicken and all the trimmings.

'I'm absolutely dying to know — have you discovered if you're really Letitia's granddaughter?' Myra asked as Tim carved the chicken.

Rhianna smiled, 'Yes, I really believe I am. It's all a bit of a mystery and I know very little. I feel sad to think that Letitia and my father didn't see each other in all those years.'

'Did she tell you why?' Myra couldn't hide her curiosity.

'Myra that's between Letitia and

Rhianna,' Tim chided his wife gently.

'Well, I haven't found out about that just yet. Thought it best to step gently. We need to build up a relationship before we exchange secrets.'

'Quite right,' Tim said approvingly. 'You don't want to rush in too quickly.'

Rhianna noticed Lawrence was keeping very quiet and suspected he probably knew what had happened all those years ago. She couldn't help wondering if it had anything to do with Anna Soames.

The conversation moved on to more general topics. Presently, Myra collected up the plates and brought in a delectable looking apple pie and ice cream.

'So what have you been up to since we saw you last, Laurie? Letitia says you've been working abroad.'

Rhianna, all ears, was amused that Myra asked such direct questions.

'Oh, I had a year in the States and then I decided to go freelance when I returned to England. I enjoy working for myself. It means I can get some painting done in between contracts.'

'Lawrence took a look at Rhianna's gallery near St Alban's,' Tim told his wife.

Myra's eyes widened. 'You've got your own gallery! How impressive is that! Well, you and Lawrence should get on well. How about that, Tim? We've got two artists in our midst. I'm sure we can use your expertise in some way.'

Lawrence laughed. 'Same old Myra — always got your eye to the main chance. She won't let us escape, you know, Rhia. So what do you want us to do?'

Myra joined in the laughter. 'Oh, I'll think of something — a talk, a workshop, an exhibition. Something to raise money for the church roof fund.'

Tim patted his wife's arm. 'I'm afraid she never gives up. You have to admire her tenacity. Give them a break, Myra. They haven't had time to catch their breath yet . . . By the way, I didn't show you where your grandfather and other ancestors were buried, did I, Rhianna? We'll have to take another look at the churchyard some time.'

'Didn't you even know your father was born in Kent?' Myra asked now.

'Well, I suppose he might have mentioned it at some time, but I can't say I took too much notice. I expect Letitia will fill me in at some point.'

'Oh, Tish will have lots of things to share with you, I'm certain of that,' Lawrence assured her.

'Such a dear little name, *Tish*, it always makes me want to say, bless you,' Myra observed.

Rhianna caught Lawrence's gaze. There was a definite twinkle in his eyes and she couldn't help laughing at Myra's comment.

Over dessert, Tim and Myra regaled them with anecdotes from their years on the mission field in Africa.

The evening passed quickly and pleasantly and Rhianna realised what a delightful couple they were. She was relieved that no more was said about

Letitia Delroy. There were masses of things she needed to know. Questions kept coming into her mind but, for that day, she had reached saturation point.

They were about to leave when Myra asked, 'Are the pair of you around tomorrow evening? It almost slipped my mind. We've got a concert in the village hall. It's very varied — the choir from the school are singing and the church choristers as well as some talented individuals. It promises to be a good evening. We wondered if we'd need to postpone it with all that's happened, but the police haven't raised any objections.'

'Perhaps Letitia would like to come,' Lawrence said. 'Do we need to get the tickets beforehand?'

He purchased three. Rhianna realised that he was a generous person, unlike Marcus, who had always seemed reluctant to put his hand in his pocket. She was determined to pay her way.

'Absolutely not,' Lawrence told her. 'It's my treat — so forget it.'

As they entered the bar, someone called out to them, 'Come and join us for a drink.'

Rhianna suddenly couldn't face any more cross questioning, besides, she wanted to phone Fiona to see how things were progressing at the gallery and so she pleaded tiredness and went upstairs.

Fiona was waiting to catch up with her news, especially in regards to Lawrence.

'Wow,' she said, 'so do you think he's trustworthy?'

'I'd like to think so. He's an interesting character and he seems to be sincere.' She decided not to mention the incident earlier that evening. Fiona would never let her live it down. Instead she told her about her visit to Letitia and what she'd learnt about the Soames family. She was subjected to a barrage of questions about Letitia.

'I can't believe you call your grand-mother, *Letitia*?'

'Well, I somehow can't bring myself

to call her *Grandmother*, yet. After all, everything's happened so quickly. I didn't even know I had a grandmother until a short time ago.'

'Well, it must be just as strange for her,' Fiona said. 'I'd make the most of her if I were you. I'd give anything to have my grandparents still around. She sounds a nice lady.'

'Mmm, I think she is, but, remember, I've only seen her for just over an hour. It's very early days yet, but I'm sure we're going to get on.' Rhianna sniffed. 'She's a lot like my father, Fi. It's making me feel very emotional . . . Anyway, can we leave it for now? Tell me about the gallery.'

'You've only been gone a couple of days, Rhia! Actually, you'll be pleased to learn I've sold another painting. That customer who came in this morning wanted a present for his sister's birthday. He raved about those landscapes.'

'Great — Matt will be pleased and the commission will come in handy. Keep up the good work.'

'So when are you coming back?' Fiona wanted to know.

'Oh, it's hard to say — not until after the weekend at any rate. Actually, I've just been invited to a concert with Laurie.'

'Oh, so it's Laurie now, is it?' Fiona teased. 'Well enjoy yourself whilst I'm slaving away,' she added good-naturedly.

'For your information, my friend, I've spent the afternoon doing some photographs for another exhibition and I'm going to do some painting from them so it's not all socialising,' Rhianna said.

'If you say so. Well, keep me informed. I want to know more about this mysterious Christina Soames.'

So do I, Rhianna told herself as she prepared for bed. It still hadn't sunk in that Lawrence had been engaged to Tina. She wondered why they had split up. There were still so many unanswered questions.

★　★　★

Rhianna spent an interesting morning with Letitia Delroy.

The elderly lady had unearthed some old photograph albums and they sat side by side on the sofa. Rhianna realised there was so much she didn't know about her father.

'Did you know my mother too?'

Letitia shook her white head. 'Sadly, no. She sounded a very nice lady. Where did he meet her?'

'Oh, at an art exhibition up in London, I believe. Neither of them said much about their early lives. They had many friends in the art world.'

'How interesting. Of course your father inherited his love of art from his father. Reg tried to discourage him — said there was no money in it, unless you were a genius. I've still got a few of Reg's paintings dotted about the place but we sold a number over the years.'

'So the painting of *Anna Soames*, was that painted by my father?'

Letitia shook her white head. 'No, dear — not your father . . . Now, how about some coffee? I must put the casserole on too or we'll never get any lunch.'

Rhianna got the distinct impression that Letitia was changing the subject and wondered why. There was definitely something she didn't understand about all this and she was convinced that it was to do with the painting.

4

After coffee, Letitia took Rhianna on a tour of the downstairs rooms with Tansy trotting along beside them. It was a gracious house which had an air of shabby grandeur.

'This place is far too big for me nowadays, but I really don't want to move until I have to,' Letitia said sadly.

Rhianna thought that the upkeep of the place must be horrendous.

'Did Laurie tell you that at one time him and Tina . . . ' Letitia trailed off, obviously wondering if she'd said too much.

'He told me they were engaged for a short while, yes,' Rhianna said.

Her grandmother looked relieved. 'Oh, I'm glad he filled you in. It makes it less awkward all round. He would have been so good for her but it wasn't to be. If that had happened they would have lived here at *Wisteria Lodge* and I expect I would have moved into the cottage.'

'The cottage?' Rhianna queried, wondering if this was something else Letitia thought she knew.

'Yes, I own a cottage in the village. It's where Laurie used to live a few years back. It's an idyllic spot but it's rented out at the moment.'

Before Rhianna had time to ask her any questions Letitia said, 'Now I'm sure you'd like to see some of your grandfather's paintings and then we might just have time to take a look at your father's old room before Laurie arrives. There's a lot of his stuff in it still. I couldn't bring myself to get rid of it.'

Rhianna followed her grandmother into the dining-room and stood looking at the oil paintings adorning the walls. Her grandfather had certainly been artistically talented, but she found his subject matter rather dull — still lives and bleak landscapes. It lacked the vivacity of her father's work and she felt a sense of disappointment.

'They're not his best,' Letitia said, as if she sensed Rhianna's thoughts. 'We sold most of those. He was quite a popular artist in his day, believe it or not. He used to get commissions. What did your father do?'

'Oh, he had commissions too mainly for offices and libraries and council buildings, but it wasn't enough to live on so he worked in a gallery up in London until he retired. He set up exhibitions, lectured, that sort of thing.'

Letitia's face was full of interest.

'I'm glad he made something of himself. I never stopped thinking about him you know — wondering how he was getting on. You can't imagine how I feel now that you're here. It means the earth to me.'

Rhianna was about to pluck up courage, ask her again what it was that had been so terrible that it had led to a lifetime separation when the doorbell chimed.

'That'll be Laurie. Can you let him in, dear? How lovely — both of you together under my roof! It's more than I could ever have dreamed of. You've made an old woman very happy.'

★　★　★

To Rhianna's delight, Letitia agreed to accompany them to the concert that evening. 'But there's one condition — that you allow me to tell everyone you're my granddaughter!'

Rhianna agreed and, that evening, found herself sitting between Lawrence and Letitia in the village hall. It was an excellent amateur event. The children from the local school were an absolute delight and the applause brought the house down.

During the interval, Lawrence valiantly fought his way to the refreshments and returned bearing coffee and biscuits.

Irene Blake came across to talk to them. 'Mavis is very much better. She's being discharged soon and is going to stay with her son and family.'

'Oh, that is good news. Such a dreadful thing to happen. What's happening about the post office?' Letitia enquired.

'Oh, it's reopening next week. They've got a retired postmaster coming to take charge of things for the time-being. Lizzie is well enough to go back to work too.'

'Any news of arrests?' Lawrence asked.

Irene shook her head. ''fraid not. They'll get clever once too often.' She looked curiously at Rhianna. 'Are you planning to stay long?'

'For another few days but I'll be returning.'

Letitia put an arm about Rhianna's shoulder. 'What you won't know, Irene, is that Rhianna here is my granddaughter,' she announced triumphantly.

Irene stared at her open-mouthed. 'But I thought your name was *Soames*.'

'That's what we decided to let people think — just until we were sure — but I'm actually Rhianna *Delroy*.'

There wasn't time for any more conversation, because, just then, Tim announced the second half of the programme.

Rhianna felt a sudden wave of happiness shoot through her. A few weeks back, she had believed she was all alone in the world and now she had a grandmother. Letitia Delroy was proving to be a delightful lady. And now there was Lawrence. She couldn't believe how things were changing for her.

As the concert neared a close, the audience were invited to join in a medley of songs from popular musicals. Rhianna decided it would be an evening to remember. Lawrence's tenor voice matched her sweet soprano.

At one point, she stole a look at him and he smiled and, reaching out, put his hand over hers. His fingers were warm and firm and made hers tingle. She reminded herself sternly that she didn't intend to let another man walk over her as Marcus had done. Besides, what did she know about him and why had he broken off his engagement with Christina Soames?

After the concert had ended to tumultuous applause, Tim came across to speak to them.

'It's great to see the three of you here tonight. Have you enjoyed it?'

They assured him that they had. 'Myra will give you a lift to church tomorrow morning — if you want to come, Letitia.'

'Oh, that's OK, I'll be more than happy to fetch my grandmother,' Rhianna told him. I'm not here for much longer and want to make the most of being in her company.'

As they dropped Letitia off at *Wisteria Lodge*, Lawrence said, 'Perhaps I could join you for church tomorrow and then the three of us could go out for lunch. I know a good pub a few miles away.'

Letitia's face lit up. 'That would be wonderful, Laurie. I've had such a lovely evening.'

★   ★   ★

'So what do you think — now you've had a chance to get to know Letitia a bit more?' Lawrence asked Rhianna carefully, as they drove back to the *White Unicorn*.

'She's a lovely lady, I can't imagine what caused my father to fall out with my grandmother but, in a way, I don't want to know. It's time to move on and it's no good dwelling in the past, is it?'

'No,' Lawrence agreed, but there was a thoughtful expression on his face masked by the darkness. He was all too aware that whatever had happened between Reg Delroy and his son had been extremely serious. Tina had tried very hard to find out what had caused the falling out, but had never succeeded in discovering the truth, as far as Lawrence was aware. He just hoped it would stay that way. There had been too much heartache for one lifetime.

As they pulled up outside the pub, Lawrence took Rhianna's hands between his.

'Thanks for this evening, Rhia. I

hope that we can continue to be friends.' Leaning across he kissed her gently on the cheek.

'It's been good,' she told him genuinely. It took every ounce of self-control to behave normally. She had no intention of letting him know the effect that kiss had had on her.

* * *

Rhianna enjoyed the church service which was quite modern and included the children. She was surprised when Lawrence had come with them. Afterwards, she found herself the centre of attention yet again as Letitia introduced her to a number of her church friends. Rhianna was aware there were a number of surprised glances and wondered if anyone in the congregation knew the reason for her father cutting himself off from his parents. If they did, they were discreet and made no comment. A couple of people did ask after Tina, however, but Lawrence merely shrugged.

'Oh, I'm afraid I'm not Tina's keeper. We parted company over two years ago and our paths don't cross anymore,' he said politely to a woman in an amazing hat.

When she'd gone, Letitia told him, 'Oh, you mustn't mind Sylvia, Laurie, she's got a heart of gold but she is one of the most inquisitive people I know.'

He grinned and took her arm, 'Besides Myra, you mean!' and Letitia chuckled.

As they came out of the church, Tim Holt turned to Rhianna.

'Don't forget I've promised to show you the most recent Delroy graves. It's a bit too chilly for you to be wandering about the churchyard, isn't it, Tish?'

She nodded. 'Perhaps we'd better leave it for another time, Tim. We're going out to lunch at the *Drunken Duck* and we've booked a table.'

'Well, have a good time.'

'I intend to,' she said cheerily and clung onto Lawrence's arm as they made their way to the car. 'They've all got enough gossip to last them for a week,' she commented, a twinkle in her eye, and Rhianna and Laurie laughed.

The *Drunken Duck* was doing a roaring trade and it didn't take Rhianna long to find out why. The food, a carvery, was excellent.

'So Laurie, have you had a chance to take a look at any properties since you've been here?' Letitia asked over their meal.

'No, I'm afraid not. I've been quite busy sorting out Ron's new website. Hopefully, tomorrow, I'll get an opportunity — although I'm not holding my breath.'

'It's a pity the cottage is occupied.'

He shook his head. 'I wouldn't want to go back there, Tish, too many memories. No, I want to start afresh. If it means waiting for the right place to turn up then I'm just going to have to be patient.'

There was something Rhianna wanted to know.

'So where are you living at the moment?'

'Not far from you in Buckingham-shire. I'm staying with my parents.'

Her heart leapt, as she realised it was possible she might see him again in the near future. All her good resolutions had gone to the wind since she'd discovered Lawrence was not her enemy. Well, a girl was entitled to change her mind, wasn't she?

'Tell me some more about your gallery, Rhianna,' Letitia said.

'Well, it's in a cottage in the high street. It's quite small, but there's an upstairs which we use for storage and, when we've got sufficient funds, we're going to expand. We hold workshops and do a few courses on decoupage — that sort of thing.'

'So what have you got in mind for expansion?'

Rhianna enthused about the ideas she and Fiona had had. How, at present, they couldn't have any one exhibition for more than a month, due to the limited amount of space.

'We've even thought about serving

teas and coffee — perhaps cakes and scones.'

Rhianna suddenly saw the stern expression on Lawrence's face. Meeting his gaze, she encountered eyes as hard as granite. She turned hot and cold. Whatever had she said to make him react like this? And it suddenly dawned on her what it might be. Surely he couldn't imagine for one minute that she was angling for some money to pay for the expansion?

She thought about the comments he had made about being protective towards Letitia. A wave of anger surged through her as she realised she was right. How dare he? She had to bite her tongue to prevent herself from challenging him there and then. Just because Christina Soames had fleeced her grandmother, he couldn't put her, Rhianna, in the same category.

Rhianna lowered her gaze so that she wouldn't have to meet his. Up until then she had been enjoying the meal but now it tasted like sawdust in her mouth. She reached for her drink and took a large sip which made her choke.

'Are you all right, dear?' Letitia asked in concern.

'Absolutely,' she assured her, when she'd got her breath back. 'It just went down the wrong way.' She reached for a tissue and wiped her streaming eyes.

Fortunately, the conversation turned to village affairs and the concert the previous evening. As they sat over coffee Letitia said, 'I was wondering. I would so much like to see Mavis Blackett. Would it be too much to ask for one of you to run me to the hospital?'

The hospital was in the opposite direction from the Drunken Duck and Rhianna offered to drive the elderly lady. Lawrence said he needed to do a couple of hours work on Ron's website that afternoon and sent his regards.

Rhianna decided she would catch up with him later and put things straight. There was no way she was going to allow him to go on thinking that she wanted to take advantage of Letitia. It sickened her to think that he had such a low opinion of her. A pity she thought, just as she was really beginning to enjoy his company.

★   ★   ★

Mavis had been moved to a medical ward. She was sitting in a chair reading the newspaper when they arrived. She greeted Letitia affectionately and looked enquiringly at Rhianna.

'This is my granddaughter, Rhianna,' Letitia told her proudly. 'I told you her name was Rhianna *Soames* but it's really Rhianna *Delroy*.'

She explained briefly and Rhianna took Mavis' hand and told her how sorry she was about what had happened.

'But Irene tells me if it hadn't been for you I might have been lying on that floor for hours and poor Lizzie was quite helpless to do anything.'

'I can't help blaming myself,' Letitia told her friend. 'If only I hadn't used the name *Soames*. I'm almost certain those men thought it was Tina.'

'Now, now, Tish. It's no good speculating. It was more than likely just opportunists.'

'Then why did they ask for me?' Rhianna asked.

Mavis shrugged. 'I have no idea. It's all a bit of a mystery, isn't it? Anyway, I'm well on the mend — so you really mustn't worry about me, either of you.' She indicated the vase of colourful blooms on the locker.

'And thank you for those lovely flowers, Rhianna. So thoughtful of you . . . I've got an unexpected holiday with my son and daughter-in-law — so that can't be bad, can it?'

Rhianna continued to think there was more to the raid than opportunists but decided to keep her thoughts to herself.

'Did they take a lot of money?' Letitia wanted to know.

'Fortunately only about three hundred pounds. It could have been a great deal worse. I've been worrying about how folk will get their pensions and benefits, but apparently, Mr Jones is going to help out until I'm fit enough to come home. I'm only sorry that I couldn't put you up, dear. I'd have liked a bit of company.'

'Well, I'll be coming to see my grandmother again,' Rhianna told her.

'But she'll be staying at *Wisteria Lodge* next time round with me. Irene Blake has offered give me a bit of help around the house.'

Mavis nodded approvingly. 'Well, I'm sure she'll do a better job than that other girl you employed. What was her name?'

'Sandra. Oh, she was alright — just a bit dizzy. I just wish I knew what had happened to her.'

'Wasn't she related to those tenants of yours in the cottage?'

'That's right. The chap, Dylan, was her brother.'

After they'd been there about half an hour, Mavis' brother and wife turned up and Letitia took this as a signal to leave. It was late afternoon by the time they arrived back at *Wisteria Lodge*. Rhianna declined Letitia's offer of a cup of tea and arranged to see her the following day. There was something she needed to do.

Lawrence was not in the bar and Rhianna marched upstairs and knocked purposefully on his door, hoping he was in. The door shot open and he stood there looking preoccupied.

'Oh, good, I needed to have a word with you, Rhia.'

'And I wanted one with you,' she told him, firmly.

He stood back and she charged into the room.

'I need to make one thing absolutely clear, Lawrence Lorimer,' she began.

He folded his arms. 'Go on.'

She took a deep breath. 'I could see what was going through your mind when we were having lunch and I was talking about the gallery and how we have plans to expand it one day.'

She could see she had taken the wind out of his sails.

'Right — so you're a mind-reader are you?' he asked in a dangerously calm voice.

He wasn't going to browbeat her. She drew herself up to her full five feet four inches and met his cool green stare.

'Don't be ridiculous. I could tell that you disapproved of the conversation — no doubt thought I was hoping that Letitia, at the very least, would offer me a loan. Go on that's what you were thinking, wasn't it?'

His green eyes narrowed. 'If you say so. Perhaps it had crossed my mind. After all, Letitia's got a reputation for being a soft touch. Tina and her friends cheated her over and over and I have no intention of standing by and letting it happen again.'

She gripped his arm furiously. 'How dare you judge me on such a short acquaintance! You know absolutely nothing about me.'

His eyes blazed. 'Exactly, but I do know Letitia Delroy far better than you. She only wants to see the good in people and, as I've told you before, I don't want to see her get hurt ever again.'

She swallowed. 'I have absolutely no intention of . . . You've misread the situation. She asked me about the gallery. I was telling her. What was I supposed to do — lie?'

He looked at her uncertainly, wondering if he had misjudged her.

'No — no, of course not. If I've misconstrued things then I'm truly sorry.'

And, suddenly, she was in his arms and his fingers were gently stroking her hair and then caressing her face and throat.

For a moment she allowed herself to enjoy the closeness. She felt safe and secure. She could feel the warmth of his body against hers, smell the freshness of his cologne, but then as his face moved towards her and his lips brushed hers, she came to her senses and pulled away.

'What do you think you're doing!' she demanded angrily and pummelled his chest. 'You men are all the same; think of one thing as being the cure for everything. Well, I've got news for you! You've picked on the wrong person!'

'So I see. Well, that's told me,' he said, frankly stunned by her reaction. She had behaved like a wildcat. 'I'm sorry. I'll mind my manners in future.'

The fight went out of her and tears trembled on her lashes. She shook her head as if to shake them away. 'You needn't think you're the only one recovering from a broken relationship,' she said and made for the door just as someone knocked on it loudly.

'Lawrence, are you there?' came Ron's voice. 'Can you come? There's been a development concerning those raiders.'

'I'm here as well — so you can tell both of us,' Rhianna told him, whipping open the door and staring at him expectantly.

Ron's pale blue eyes were bulging with excitement.

'They've arrested that couple from your grandmother's cottage, Rhianna.

It probably explains why Sandra left — the girl who helped her round the house. She was the fellow's sister. Anyway, I reckon the police will be wanting to question Mrs Delroy and thought you might like to warn her, Lawrence.'

'We'll both go,' Rhianna said, before he had a chance to reply. 'Give me five minutes.'

She dashed to the bathroom and splashed water on her face and ran a comb through her hair. She needed to look composed.

Lawrence was sitting on the window-seat on the landing waiting for her. It was as if the episode between them hadn't happened. There were more important things to think about for the moment and they had to put their own differences to one side.

*   *   *

'The police have just phoned,' Letitia told them when they arrived. 'You've no idea how relieved I am to see the pair of you. Whatever is going to happen next?'

Over copious cups of tea the story was pieced together. The police officers were very patient with Letitia who was visibly shaken.

'Sandra was a willing enough girl and did her job to the best of her ability but after she'd left, I suddenly discovered several things had gone missing. Nothing of that much value — just trinkets — but it was upsetting all the same. It explains how those — those people knew Rhianna was going to be staying at the Post Office. Sandra must have overheard me talking on the phone to Mrs Blackett.'

'Our belief is she thought it was Christina Soames you were talking about,' the police officer said quietly.

Letitia sighed. 'Tina, well, yes, the thought had crossed my mind, but she's in Australia and anyway, what would they want with her?'

'That's what we'd like to know, but she obviously knew them,' he said sternly. 'She was seen visiting them at

94

the cottage. I have to tell you, Mrs Delroy that Christina Soames hasn't arrived in Australia. We actually have reason to believe she's still in England, so if you do hear from her, please get in touch on this number.'

After the police had gone, Letitia sank onto the sofa and Tansy jumped on her lap. Letitia stroked her absently.

'Whatever do they want with Tina?' she asked tiredly. 'Oh, Laurie, it never stops where that young woman is concerned. Whatever has she got herself mixed up with now?'

'It might not be anything,' he said soothingly, 'just that she obviously knew those two at the cottage and it was apparent they were anxious to find her for some reason.'

It sounded weird to Rhianna and, even as Lawrence uttered the words, she could tell that he was unconvinced. He was obviously just trying to placate Letitia.

'That Sandra must have known what was going on. That's obviously why she left. I wonder what sort of state they've left the cottage in. I'll have to get all the locks changed, won't I, Laurie?' Letitia said worriedly.

'Now, you're not to worry about all that. We'll take a look tomorrow and sort things out, won't we, Rhianna?'

'What? Oh, yes, of course, although probably the police will be taking a look too so we might not get the opportunity.'

Lawrence nodded his head. 'Ron is absolutely in his element. There's never been so much excitement in Brookhurst and it's drawing in the punters.'

Letitia suddenly brightened. 'Well, stay and have some tea now that you're here. Mrs Dalton gave me such a lovely lemon drizzle cake when she visited the other day. There's ham and bread in the fridge. I'm sure you could make a few sandwiches, Rhianna.'

Rhianna, glad of an opportunity to escape went off to the kitchen. If Ron thought he was having a lot of excitement he ought to be in her shoes. She

96

didn't seem to have time to sort out one situation before the next one arose.

She busied herself making sandwiches and finding a plate for the cake. She was beginning to feel a little foolish regarding Lawrence. She knew that the problem was that she was extremely vulnerable and that it would be all too easy to rush headlong into another relationship and get hurt all over again.

Lawrence was a devastatingly attractive man. She had to concede with Fiona on that point. She was aware of a certain magnetism; those green eyes that changed with his mood, the touch of his hand on hers and the rich chestnut hair falling over his forehead. To say nothing of his physique!

She pulled herself together sharply. No, she would not allow herself to get involved. It would only lead to more heartache. If she'd let him kiss her, she knew there would be no turning back. It would be like being sucked into a whirlpool from which there was no escape and she had no intention of letting that happen.

The subject of her thoughts appeared in the doorway at that moment.

He saluted. 'Reporting for duty, Ma'am. I've been sent to carry in the plates.'

She had to smile. 'It's all ready. She indicated the laden tray. 'I've just got the tea to make.'

'It's years since I ate a proper Sunday tea,' he told her, a twinkle in his eyes. 'Sorry you've been forced to endure even more of my company.'

The colour tinged her cheeks. It was now or never.

'No, I'm sorry, Laurie. I don't know what came over me. It's just that everything's happening so quickly.'

His expression softened. 'I know and you are finding it all a bit much. Well, let's hope we can sort things out quickly at the cottage and then I suspect you'll be wending your way home.'

She nodded. 'Fiona's trying to organise some workshops and she'll need my input. It wouldn't be fair for me to leave her too long. There's the online business as well.'

'Yes, and I've got a few other calls to make too. Things that I postponed in order to come here.' He stretched out his hand.

'I hope we can part on good terms.'

She took his hand and caught her breath at the contact. 'Absolutely. I'm grateful to you for looking out for my grandmother,' she told him. It felt as if her hand was being scorched. 'The kettles' boiling,' she said and turned away, her heart heavy.

5

The following morning Rhianna accompanied Lawrence to the cottage. There was still an official presence — presumably, the CID Rhianna decided — and so they weren't allowed in.

'We'll be finished in a day or so. I'm afraid it's in a bit of a mess, but there's no structural damage,' one of the men said.

'Poor Letitia. It seems to be one thing after another,' Rhianna said, feeling a surge of sympathy for her grandmother.

'Certainly does,' Lawrence agreed. 'Well, there's not much point hanging around here, is there? Nothing we can do for the moment.'

She shook her head and stood for a minute looking at the whitewashed cottage with its green shutters. The flower borders were a mass of snowdrops and yellow crocuses and already green daffodil spikes were poking through the soil.

'It's very picturesque, isn't it?'

Lawrence had a faraway look in his eye.

'Yes, you should just see it in the summer when the roses are climbing up that trellis. It's enchanting then. Absolutely chocolate box.'

'I can imagine.' She hesitated and then said in a rush, 'I've arranged to see Letitia this afternoon. Perhaps I'll take a walk before then — unless, didn't you say you intended to look at some properties this morning?'

'Yeah — why, do you fancy coming with me?' Lawrence seemed pleased. 'You'd get to see a bit more of Brookhurst that way.'

'Why not?' She tried to sound casual. 'I'm only sorry that I can't help with the clearing up here, but I've told Fiona I'll be returning on Wednesday at the latest. We've got a workshop on Friday. I've no idea how she's set it up so quickly, but that's Fiona for you.'

'What sort of workshop?' He appeared genuinely interested.

101

'Pottery decorating. It's the school's half-term. We've had one before and it proved popular. The children choose plates, mugs or dishes all in plain white and then they personalise them. It's good fun.'

'Sounds it. I'm all for anything creative and hands on for youngsters. It's far better than them being stuck in front of a computer all day.'

'Absolutely,' she agreed. 'They leave their stuff with us for a couple of days to finish off in the kiln and then it's ready to use. The kiddies come with their parents who seem to enjoy it equally as much.'

Lawrence looked thoughtful. 'And do they just turn up or must they book?'

'Some do but it's pretty informal. We have several sessions so if one's full they wait for the next. Actually, it's a bit chaotic.' She laughed. 'Noisy and messy.'

'I'm full of admiration. You girls certainly have a wealth of ideas.'

She grinned. 'We have to — it's a

question of survival. We don't charge much per head. It's a lot cheaper than buying things from the shops. The children might like to make something for a present. We've got *Mothers' Day* and *Easter* coming up soon.'

'Don't worry about the cleaning at the cottage,' he told her as they reached the car. 'I'll ask Ron. He's bound to have some contacts. I'll sort it out. It's unfortunate poor Tish chose the wrong tenants.'

This time he took a different route. It was very scenic in spite of the time of the year. The hedgerows had quantities of evergreen ivy and old man's beard clinging to them. Here and there a scarlet hip remained undiscovered by the birds. Suddenly, he slowed down to allow some riders to pass.

'There's a riding school over there. And there are quite a few farms dotted about. Which reminds me — we could stop at the local farm shop on the way back. I'll give Tish a ring — see if she wants any supplies.'

'Are you planning to stay in Brookhurst for a while longer?'

She tried to make the question sound casual.

He shook his head. 'No, I'm afraid I can't. Family commitments — I've promised to return home by the end of the week. But I'll be back to see Tish from time to time . . . What have you decided?'

'Oh, I imagine I'll be spending quite a bit of time here in the future. I'm not going to drop Letitia. She's a lovely lady. Besides, there's a lot I need to find out about in this area. I haven't even had a chance to look at my ancestors' graves yet. So, Brookhurst will feature quite prominently in my life from now on.'

Lawrence smiled. 'That's great. I hoped you'd say that.'

She felt a warm glow inside her and hoped he meant it. She stole a glance at him, liking the way his chestnut hair fell across his brow and noting his strong profile.

'Letitia and I have such a lot of catching up to do . . . Do you suppose she might like to see the gallery?' she asked presently.

He nodded. 'She most probably would, but I think you need to take things slowly. Letitia hasn't left Brookhurst for more than the occasional day for several years now.'

'Mmm, I'd thought of that. It is possible to do Herts in a day but it would be quite tiring — oh, goodness there's a pheasant in that field!'

He shot a look at her. 'You're obviously a girl after my own heart. You enjoy the countryside?'

'I certainly do — now where are these properties you've brought me to see?'

'There's one just round here somewhere. It's a bit further out than I'd thought, but we'll take a look whilst we're here. I haven't got an appointment but, apparently, it's OK just to turn up.'

They walked along a muddy lane and eventually came across the house which appeared rather neglected. Lawrence looked at it in dismay.

'Well, I was told it was in need of some refurbishment but it looks more run down than I expected.'

He rang the bell and a dog started barking. After a while, the door was flung open by a large woman with iron-grey hair, wearing a grubby apron and clutching a rolling pin.

'Yes?' she asked abruptly.

'We wondered if it was convenient to look round your house?' Lawrence asked politely.

The woman scowled. 'No, it is not and I'll tell you for why. My daughter persuaded us to put it on the market, but we've changed our minds. We withdrew it this morning — isn't that right, Alf?'

A small wizened little man, wearing a multi-coloured, woollen hat, came to stand beside his wife. He solemnly nodded, but didn't say a word. Rhianna bit her lip to prevent herself from giggling.

'Well, we're so sorry to have troubled you,' Lawrence said pleasantly.

'Right. Good-day to you.' And the woman practically slammed the door shut in their faces.

It was too much for Rhianna who, seeing the amusement in Lawrence's eyes, gave a whoop of laughter. 'He looked like a little garden gnome,' she spluttered and he joined in.

'I was a bit worried about that rolling pin,' he said, wiping his eyes. 'Do you suppose she uses it to keep her husband in check?'

This set Rhianna laughing again. It eased the tension she'd been feeling for the past few days. She was enjoying Lawrence's company more than she could have imagined.

The garden path was muddy and, at one point, she slipped and would have fallen, but Lawrence caught her arm and retained it. The contact was electric and she caught her breath, wondering if he were aware of it too.

When they arrived back at the car Lawrence said, 'There is one other property I can view on the way back to

Brookhurst. I know the owners and I've got a proper appointment this time — for eleven o'clock.'

Jill and Tom Yates were very different from the previous couple.

'You're Letitia's granddaughter. Well, that's one in the eye for Tina,' Jill remarked, as they sat over coffee in the elegant but minimally furnished sitting-room.

'Why would you say that?' Rhianna asked, startled.

'Oh, I should have thought that was obvious. You're the official next of kin — so you stand to inherit *Wisteria Lodge* and everything that goes with it.'

There was a shocked silence and then Tom said, 'You must excuse my wife's bluntness, Rhianna. I'm afraid Tina rather blotted her copy book — as far as Jill was concerned — as Lawrence knows.'

Lawrence chose to ignore this comment. He drained his cup and looked pointedly at the clock.

'Well, we'd better press on,' Tom said taking the hint. 'Let's start with the kitchen, shall we?'

Rhianna followed in a daze. Did everyone think the same as Jill — that she had an ulterior motive for tracking down her grandmother — ultimate financial gain? Was that what Lawrence thought too?

'I'm surprised you're thinking of moving back here,' Jill said, as they stood looking at the beautifully appointed but very clinical kitchen in white and stainless steel.

'Oh, I think Brookhurst has got a certain charm all of its own,' he told her. 'Anyway, I've made a lot of friends here.'

Presently, as they wandered round the landscaped garden, Lawrence said, 'The problem is that nothing will ever compare with the cottage. It was perfect.'

'And you really wouldn't consider living there again?'

His face had a closed expression. 'No, there are too many memories.'

She nodded, realising that he didn't want to talk about it. Lawrence told the Yateses that he'd be in touch and they retraced their steps to the car.

'Let's get one thing straight, Lawrence,' Rhianna told him as she buckled up her seat belt. 'I'm not a gold-digger. I didn't visit my grandmother in the hopes she'd leave me anything. For all I knew she was a pauper.'

'She's hardly that, but she's not wealthy either.' He squeezed her arm. 'You mustn't mind Jill. She speaks her mind, and I suppose it is a pretty unusual situation you turning up out of the blue like this.'

Rhianna had to agree. 'But the point is that Letitia contacted me and not the other way round.'

'Yes, I realise that and eventually everyone else will too.'

On the way back, Lawrence pointed out the farm shop and, seeing there was a café, Rhianna had an idea.

'I wonder if Letitia would like a spin out this afternoon — then she could select her own produce and I could take her for tea.'

'That's a wonderful idea. I'd offer to

join you but I've arranged to see a mate of Ron's who's got a problem with his computer.'

When they arrived back at *The White Unicorn*, Rhianna looked at her watch.

'Have you got time for a quick lunch — my treat?'

To her secret delight he agreed and they sat in at a quiet corner table enjoying bowls of steaming soup and chunks of crusty bread.

'So what shall I tell Letitia about the cottage?' she asked, breaking off a piece of bread.

'Oh, just say it's all in hand so she's no need to worry. I'll explain everything tomorrow when I call to see her. Can't be specific but it'll be sometime in the afternoon.'

He leant towards her and lowered his voice.

'Rhianna, that picture your grand-mother asked you about — the portrait of Anna Soames . . .'

She looked at him spoon poised. 'What about it? If you know something tell me, because I've got a feeling it holds a clue to a lot of things I don't understand.'

He helped himself to more bread. 'Yes, I'm sure you're right, but I'm afraid I don't know any more than you — except your grandmother is most anxious that you keep it safe.'

'Why? Whatever can be so important about it? She can have the wretched thing for all I care. Do you know who painted it?'

He had a good idea but preferred not to say anything until he was sure.

'Tish doesn't want the painting at *Wisteria Lodge*. She thinks it's best if you keep it in your possession for the time-being.'

Rhianna was suddenly tired of the whole affair.

'I've a good mind to get rid of it,' she told him.

'No — no don't do that,' he said more loudly than he intended — so that people on the next table looked in their direction.

They lapsed into silence and then he said quietly, 'Rhianna, if ever you feel in trouble, feel free to ring me. You can reach me on my mobile.'

She felt that odd little shiver of fear again.

'Trouble — why should I . . . ?' But she took the card he proffered and stowed it carefully in her handbag. 'Thanks, I'll do that.'

Presently, he got to his feet. 'Thanks for the soup, Rhia. It really hit the spot. Now I must dash but I'll see you at breakfast tomorrow.'

She felt an unexpected pang of disappointment that he couldn't accompany them that afternoon. She sat there for a few minutes staring into space and wondering what exactly he had been warning her about.

* * *

That afternoon was a lovely nostalgic trip down memory lane for Letitia. Periodically, Rhianna parked the car so that her grandmother could point something out to her.

'That field over there is where Joe had a picnic with his friends on his tenth birthday. We knew the farmer, you see. It was such a happy occasion. It was a sunny July day and the children were in their element. Afterwards, they had a game of rounders.'

As she looked across the field, Rhianna could almost see the children running about and hear their laughter.

'So, did Dad go to the local school?' she wanted to know.

'Oh, yes, and he passed the eleven plus and went to the grammar. He was such a bright child . . . Oh, look there's the little stream where the kiddies came to paddle and fish. They caught quantities of those tiny things — *tid-dlers* they called them, but they threw them back.'

On the way to the farm shop they stopped yet again — this time so that Letitia could point out a wood.

'I often used to bring your father here

when he was a boy. We had such lovely rambles. It's abundant in wildlife and your father loved it here. One evening, we stayed out later than we intended and we came across a family of badgers playing beneath the trees.'

In her mind's eye, Rhianna could visualise the scene.

'Your grandfather and I did our courting here,' Letitia confided, her eyes lighting up as the memories flooded back. 'In spring there are primroses and later, in May, bluebells like a sea of shimmering blue. You'll have to come here with your paint-brush, Rhianna.'

'Who needs a paintbrush when you've painted such a wonderful word picture,' she told her grandmother with a smile.

'I taught your father to value the simple things in life.'

'And he always did,' Rhianna assured her. 'Now I know where he got his love of nature from. He passed it on to me. We went for long country walks too.'

Presently, they pulled up at the farm shop.

'Now, the big barn at the back is still used for dances in the summer. That's where your father used to go when he was a teenager . . . '

Letitia trailed off and Rhianna wondered if she had been about to mention who he'd taken to those dances. Her father had been a good-looking man, so it would come as no surprise to her to learn that there had been other girlfriends before he'd met her mother. But, Rhianna knew that from the time he'd met her mother, she had been the one true love of his life.

They wandered round the shop and Letitia took pleasure in selecting her fruit and vegetables. Rhianna made a few purchases too and stowed them in the boot of her car.

The café at the farm-shop overlooked an orchard. It was a pleasant place serving traditional afternoon teas.

'I haven't been here for ages,' Letitia said, as she buttered her scone.

'I think Tina and Laurie brought me on one occasion. It was summer and we sat out on the terrace. It's such a peaceful spot, isn't it?'

'It certainly is,' Rhianna agreed, again wondering why Tina and Lawrence had split up. She sounded a restless, discontented sort of person used to getting her own way.

'Life throws up unexpected surprises sometimes, doesn't it Rhianna? I've had such a delightful few days and I'm going to miss you dreadfully when you go home.'

'Oh, I'll miss you too, Letitia,' Rhianna assured her, 'But now that we've found each other, we'll keep in touch.'

She was going to miss Lawrence too, she decided, but that was a different matter entirely.

★ ★ ★

On Wednesday morning, Lawrence encountered Rhianna trundling her suitcase along the corridor towards the stairs.

'Hi, can I carry that for you or are you one of those independent feminist types who prefer to grit their teeth and carry on — even if it kills them?'

Rhianna laughed. 'I certainly am, but that doesn't mean to say I don't appreciate help when it comes to negotiating winding staircases.'

He picked up the case and carried it effortlessly downstairs and out to her car.

'I hope we'll be seeing more of each other in the future, Rhia.' And, stooping, he kissed her gently on the cheek.

'Yes, I hope so too,' she told him, resisting the urge to reach up and touch the spot where his lips had been.

He stood there waving as she drove away and she fancied her heartbeat quickened.

★   ★   ★

When Rhianna arrived at *Wisteria Lodge*, Irene whipped open the door.

'Did you catch up with that guy who was looking for you?' she wanted to know.

Rhianna stared at her fearfully. 'What guy?'

'That reporter chap. He interviewed Mavis just as she was leaving the hospital and came into the post office and saw Lizzie and me, but we didn't know where you were.'

Rhianna gasped with relief. 'Irene you nearly gave me a heart attack. I thought you meant someone more sinister.'

'Sorree — his mate took oceans of pictures. Fame at last! Mind you, I wouldn't like to go through that again in a hurry!'

'Nor me,' Rhianna said with a shiver.

Letitia was in the sitting-room, Tansy on her lap.

'Oh, I'm so glad you've come. I've sorted out a couple of keepsakes you might like to have, dear. Things that belonged to your father.'

She handed Rhianna a flat package. 'Save it to open until you get home. I wanted to show you his room, but it'll keep until we're alone.'

They chatted about a variety of things and, presently, Irene brought in a tray of coffee. She refused to stay and have a cup with them, saying she needed to pick up Lizzie's small son from nursery shortly.

'Irene's an absolute treasure,' Letitia told Rhianna when she'd gone. 'She's agreed to come up here a couple of mornings a week to help me out, as I believe I told you. I think it'll work out really well.'

It was a tearful parting. Letitia hugged Rhianna who told her, 'I'll be back before you know it and — when I come next time — I'll bring you some prints of the photographs I've taken.'

Letitia smiled and wiped away a tear. 'Well, I've got Laurie coming to see me this afternoon. I'm so fortunate. Only a short while ago I had no-one in my life and now I've got the pair of you.'

Rhianna hugged her back. 'I feel the same way,' she told her sincerely. 'I thought I was the last of the line when Dad died, but now I've discovered I've got a grandmother.'

She kissed the elderly lady and made more promises to come again.

6

The drive back to Hertfordshire was uneventful. Rhianna decided to pop into the gallery on the way home.

'Am I pleased to see you,' Fiona told her. 'It's been manic here.'

Rhianna poured some coffee and they sat down at one of the tables. Fiona gave her an update on what had been happening during the past few days and filled her in about Friday's workshop.

'We've still got several boxes of mugs and plates left over from last time and I've ordered more eggcups and dishes. The suppliers assure me they'll be here on time. We've been inundated with requests — oh and Matthew's sold another painting.'

Rhianna's eyes widened. 'Another one! Wow! He will be pleased. His work is proving popular.'

'Certainly is . . . Now, before you tell me all about your trip, you'd better listen to this . . . We've had one or two weird phone calls,' Fiona informed her.

A shiver ran along Rhianna's spine. 'What sort of weird?'

'Asking for Ms Soames. I told the first caller firmly that no one of that name was here, but the second one was more persistent so I put the phone down.'

Rhianna gasped. 'Oh, my goodness! This is a nightmare! If only Letitia hadn't called me *Soames*. I'm sure that's why people keep asking for me.'

'I'm afraid that's not all — there was a visitor,' Fiona said dramatically.

Rhianna frowned. 'How d'you mean — *a visitor*? We often have visitors.'

'This one was from the press — the chap said he had a friend in Kent who'd obviously tipped him off about the raid — wanted to know where Miss Soames was. Don't worry; I didn't give you away — stuck to my story.'

'Thanks. So those people who

phoned up — were they from the press too?'

Fiona spread her hands. 'Possibly — no idea ... Anyway, let's forget about it. Look, why don't you come round to supper at mine tonight? Dave's got a darts match with his mates.'

Rhianna suddenly felt tired. The emotional time of last few days was catching up with her.

'Thanks but there are a few things I ought to do.'

Seeing Fiona's disappointed face she said, 'Tell you what — come to me. We'll have a take-away and some more catch-up time.'

'OK — and you can tell me all about the gorgeous Laurie.'

* * *

The gorgeous Laurie was sharing a tray of tea with Letitia, even as Fiona spoke.

'She's a truly lovely girl, Laurie,' Letitia told him warmly.

He nodded, 'She certainly seems to be. I'm pleased it's working out for you.'

'It seems Joe hadn't said anything to her about what happened all those years ago,' she said slowly.

'And I take it you haven't told her either?' he prompted gently.

She twisted her hands in her lap. 'No, not yet. We need to get to know each other a bit more before then. Our relationship is still rather — fragile.'

He gave her a searching glance. 'And is ours, Tish?'

Her head shot up. 'No, of course not — whatever makes you say that, Laurie? Oh, I think I see where you're coming from.'

He nodded. 'You didn't tell myself or Tina what caused the rift between Rhianna's father and Reg.'

There was sadness in her eyes. She stroked Tansy absently.

'No — well, sometimes things are best left unsaid, and it was all a long time ago. There was enough upset then and I don't want it to happen again.'

He nodded. 'I understand your sentiments, but I suspect that this time you might have to rake up the past in order to move forward.'

Letitia knew that he was talking sense. She sighed. 'Yes, maybe you're right. Oh, dear some decisions can be very difficult, can't they?'

'Absolutely — such as who's going to have that last scone. Shall we cut it in half?'

* * *

When Rhianna got home, she had an urge to go upstairs to look at the picture of Anna Soames. It was beginning to hold a strange fascination for her. It was already dark and the attic was not well lit, so she decided to wait for another day.

She unpacked, sorted out a pile of laundry for the wash and leafed through the mail which was mainly junk.

She was just about to ring her grandmother when she suddenly remembered the keepsake Letitia had given her. It would be better to take a look first so that she could thank her properly.

She made a cup of tea and curled up on the sofa. She opened the package carefully. Inside, she found a sketchbook, a thick school exercise book labelled in bold writing, *Joseph Delroy, Nature Study*, and a pen and pencil set engraved with her father's name.

The tears flowed as she examined them. All these years her grandmother had kept them. Had she hoped that one day she would be reunited with her son?

The sketches mostly had dates on the bottom and had obviously been from her father's art college days. There were two or three pencil drawings of a very lovely young woman and Rhianna didn't need to be told that the model was Anna Soames.

As she closed the book a photograph fell out. It was of a group of young people all laughing at some joke. She didn't recognise any of them at first, and then she picked out her father and, standing next to him, an attractive woman who had to be Anna. On the other side of her was Henry Parsons, Rhianna's godfather.

When she turned the photograph over she discovered a list of names which confirmed she'd guessed accurately.

After a while, she picked up the phone to her grandmother.

'Hallo, Letitia. Just to let you know I got back safely.'

'That's good. Oh, I've had such a lovely afternoon chatting with Laurie — he's only just gone. I hadn't realised how late it was. How was your journey, dear?'

'Fine — Letitia thank you so much for the keepsakes. I'll really treasure them — especially the photograph?'

'Photograph? What photograph, dear?' Letitia sounded puzzled.

'The one that was in the sketchbook. It's got a number of names on the back, but the only people I recognise are my father, Anna Soames and Henry Parsons.'

'Well, fancy that. I must have overlooked it. Henry Parsons — I remember him really well. He was one of your father's friends from Art College. He often came to stay. So they kept in touch, did they?'

'Yes, until I was about twelve. Henry was my godfather — still is, I suppose, but he and his wife live in New Zealand now.'

'Really — he was such a nice young man. And you say there are names on the back of this photograph. Would you read them out to me, dear?'

Rhianna obliged and periodically her grandmother stopped her and told her a bit about the people she remembered.

'Well, of course you already know a bit about Anna. They were all friends together but most of them have moved away from Brookhurst now.'

★   ★   ★

It was a strange feeling, Rhianna thought, as she tidied away and ordered a Chinese takeaway. All these people her father had once known and she had never heard of. Of course, there was Henry Parsons. Perhaps she would email him sometime.

Oh Dad — if only you were around so that you could tell me what happened all those years ago. It must have been pretty bad to make you pretend to us that you no longer had any parents.

As they sat over their Chinese meal, Fiona filled her in a bit more about the online business and what else had been going on at the gallery.

'I've had a few enquiries about your decoupage classes. People wanting to make cards for *Mother's Day* or *Easter*. It's a golden opportunity, Rhia. Couldn't you do a taster class perhaps?'

'That's a great idea. You're a genius, Fi.'

'Now it's your turn,' Fiona said when they had finalised the arrangements for

Friday and she'd told her friend about a couple of outings she'd had with Dave. 'I want a blow by blow account of what happened.'

Rhianna helped herself to some more sweet and sour chicken and gave her an edited version. Fiona's eyes widened as she mentioned the CID searching the cottage.

'And you're still none the wiser about why your father cut himself off from his parents?' she asked at length.

'Nope. But I'm just wondering if my godfather in New Zealand might know anything. I was only a small girl when he emigrated and we only contact each other at Christmas usually, but he was a friend of Dad's.'

'On the other hand, it might be best to let sleeping dogs lie,' Fiona said cryptically. 'But you can tell me about the gorgeous Laurie. Now that you've discovered he's not the enemy . . . did you see much of him?'

It was an unfortunate choice of words. A little smile played about

Rhianna's lips, as she thought of her encounter with Lawrence outside the bathroom at *The White Unicorn*. She'd seen a fair bit of him then!

'What?' Fiona demanded, chopsticks suspended on the way to her mouth.

'Well, there was one incident . . . '

Fiona was all agog but Rhianna told her about the episode at the house they went to visit and the woman with the rolling pin

Fiona gave her knowing look. 'Why do I get the feeling you're holding out on me? You were staying in the same pub. Did you eat with him?'

Rhianna nodded. 'We had a meal at the Vicarage. Tim and Myra Holt are a really great couple.'

Fiona threw a handful of prawn crackers at her friend in exasperation.

'That wasn't what I meant and you know it!'

'Oh, Laurie and I got on well enough. But we haven't known each other for more than five minutes.'

Suddenly Rhianna didn't want to

discuss Laurie. She swept up the empty containers and took them into the kitchen.

When she returned with coffee and a couple of chocolate mousses that she'd found lurking at the back of the fridge, approaching their sell by date, Fiona was leafing through the sketchbook Letitia had given her.

'These are quite something, aren't they Rhia? Would you consider having another exhibition of your father's work sometime?'

'Possibly, but that sketchbook wouldn't be included. It's too precious.'

She plucked it from Fiona's hands and placed it on the table.

Their conversation turned to lighter topics and, presently, Fiona jumped to her feet. 'I said I'd join Dave and the guys for a drink at the pub. Their match should be over by now. Fancy coming with me?'

Rhianna declined and, after Fiona had left, took yet another look at the sketches of Anna Soames, as if by doing so she could find the answer to the puzzle that seemed to be niggling away at the back of her mind.

Her parents had always had such a good loving relationship and the three of them had been a complete family. She had never had any reason to question anything about her father's past before, but now one or two doubts were creeping in and she wished they would go away.

* * *

On Friday morning, Rhianna and Fiona stood looking around them. The gallery was all set up for the workshop. They had sufficient spaces for twenty children and a number of adults.

'Well, we're all prepared,' Fiona said, peering out of the window. 'Stand back ready for take-off. Here they come!'

Rhianna enjoyed these sessions. It was lovely watching the joy on the children's' faces when they'd achieved something creative. Several of the parents, mostly mums, congregated at one end of the gallery for a chat over coffee; others joined in with their offspring.

A number of the children had been before and, after a brief talk from Rhianna and Fiona, settled busily to their tasks. Most had plenty of ideas and those who got stuck were provided with sheets of designs to trace or copy. It was a noisy, happy atmosphere, well organised and yet informal.

Rhianna had just come back downstairs with a couple of boxes of supplies. As she reached the bottom step, she saw Fiona settling a small chestnut-haired girl on a stool. Lawrence was smiling down at her.

Taken aback, Rhianna set the boxes down on the end of the table.

'Hi, Rhia. This is Katie,' Lawrence told her and turned to the child. 'I told you you'd be having a fun time this morning, didn't I?'

The little girl, absorbed in what was going on around her, merely nodded.

Rhianna's head was whirling and, as soon as was possible, she busied herself on the other side of the room. Why hadn't Lawrence told her he had a child? Now she came to think of it he had mentioned family commitments. Surely the little girl couldn't be his and Tina's? If so then he had to know where she was. Rhianna dismissed that thought almost immediately, as being too incredulous.

Once or twice she caught Lawrence looking in her direction and bent her head to speak with a child. After a while, Lawrence went to have a coffee and she crossed to Katie's side. The little girl looked up at her and beamed. Judging from her gappy teeth she had to be around seven.

'I choosed flowers for Mummy, but I don't know what to do for Daddy,' Katie confided.

'No problem. I've got some sheets of patterns to help you decide. I'm sure you'll find plenty to choose from.'

Katie was a dear little girl and

Rhianna was incensed. Why couldn't Lawrence have mentioned that he had a child? For all she knew, he'd gone back to her mother after he'd left Tina. How dare he flirt with Rhianna when there was someone else in his life?

She moved away to help a small boy who hadn't a clue what he was doing. When she next looked up, she saw a couple of men standing in the doorway. One was carrying a camera. The press had turned up. Rhianna had completely forgotten they were coming and Fiona was nowhere to be seen.

Rhianna had a brief word with the reporter and photographer, and then she clapped her hands for attention and explained what was happening; giving the parents the opportunity to withdraw their children to the back of the gallery if they didn't want them to be photographed. To her relief, Fiona reappeared just then carrying a bundle of design sheets.

The thought of being in the news-paper made the children's day. The photographer took some pictures of Matthew's paintings too, which was a bonus.

'Are you sure you weren't mixed up in that raid?' the reporter asked Rhianna. 'Only my mate was telling me . . . '

Rhianna shook her head. 'Now, if you don't mind we really must press on. We've another group of children coming in shortly. I look forward to reading your article next Friday.'

As the workshop came to an end and Fiona began to collect up the pottery in carefully labelled trays, Rhianna noticed that Katie looked upset and went over to see what the problem was. Apparently, the little girl hadn't realised she couldn't take her mugs home with her there and then.

Katie's lip trembled, 'But I wanted to give it to Mummy for *Mothers' Day*.'

Lawrence hunkered down to her level. 'Don't worry, Pumpkin, I'll collect your mugs for you next week — promise. You'll have it in plenty of time.'

He popped them into the tray and

unknotted Katie's apron.

Rhianna realised how good he was with children. She left him and went to help another girl who hadn't quite finished her pattern. When Rhianna next looked up, she saw Lawrence was in earnest conversation with Fiona, and Katie was putting on her coat.

'I'll pop in on Tuesday afternoon to collect the mugs — if that's OK,' he told them.

'I'm impressed with the way you two organised this workshop. The kids were so enthusiastic and involved.'

Fiona did a mock curtsey. 'Thank you kind sir — we aim to please.'

She began clearing up and settling one or two children who had arrived for the next session. Katie tugged Lawrence's arm.

'Come on. We mustn't be late for Grandma and Mummy.'

He looked at Rhianna apologetically. 'We've arranged to meet up for a family lunch. Talk about a petticoat govern-ment! OK, young Katie, say thank you to Rhia and Fiona.'

They were so busy for the rest of the morning that Rhianna didn't have time to think, but there was a heavy feeling in the pit of her stomach. As they snatched a short lunch break before the older children came in that afternoon Fiona challenged her.

'Rhia, whatever was wrong between you and Laurie? You were avoiding him for most of the session.'

Rhianna gulped down a mouthful of coffee; it burnt her tongue.

'I should have thought that was obvious. Can't you guess? He didn't tell me he had a child and possibly an ex-wife or partner — other than Tina. He's having lunch with Katie's mother now, even as we speak. He must be a right Lothario.'

Fiona stood staring at her and then began to laugh.

'Oh Rhianna — talk about crossed wires! Katie's not his daughter, she's his niece!'

Rhianna gasped and clapped her

hand to her mouth. 'Oh, my goodness. What a fool I've been. Whatever must he think?'

Fiona shook her head in bemusement. 'What I don't understand Rhia is would it have mattered if he had a child?'

Rhianna gaped at her, 'Absolutely not. You know I like children. Katie's a sweet little girl, whoever her mother is. It's just that I prefer people to be upfront with me.'

Fiona gave her friend a slap on the back. 'So you do care about the gorgeous Laurie? You're not quite impervious to his charms! Go on admit it!'

Rhianna knew it was difficult to keep things from her friend, but she had no intention of admitting anything. She fixed her with a reproving look.

'Stop reading things into the situation, Fi. I haven't known Laurie more than five minutes . . . Now, we'd better get organised for this afternoon. Those teenagers can be rather demanding if we don't keep on top of things.'

As she checked that they'd got everything ready, she wondered miserably how she could put things right with Lawrence.

★ ★ ★

Lawrence was eating lunch with his family in a restaurant in St Albans.

'I liked that lady with the gold hair. She helped me with my pattern,' Katie said, spearing a chip.

'Who's this?' Lawrence's sister-in-law, Allison asked.

'Katie means Rhianna who runs the gallery with her friend Fiona.'

'She was nice too,' Katie piped up. 'She's got red hair and she's funny. Can we go there again, Uncle Laurie, please?'

'Oh, I'm sure we can when you come to stay with Grandma and Grandpa another time ... Rhianna is Letitia Delroy's granddaughter,' he explained to Allison.

Allison's eyebrows shot up. 'Didn't

know Letitia had any family.'

'Tell you later,' Mary Lorimer mouthed, nodding slightly towards Katie.

But Katie was blowing bubbles in her lemonade and not listening.

'Don't do that,' Allison chided her small daughter. 'You still haven't told me what you made at the workshop.'

Katie sighed and rolled her eyes. 'I told you, Mummy. It's a surprise. You'll have to be pa-chent,' she said, trying out a word her mother often used on her.

The two women tried to keep straight faces.

'Well, she's a chip off the old block and no mistake,' Mary Lorimer said. She turned to Laurie who was still trying to figure out why Rhianna had given him the cold shoulder. He had no idea what he could have done to offend her. He frowned. Perhaps he should ring her and try to find out.

'Laurie what on earth's wrong?' his mother demanded. 'This is supposed to be an enjoyable family meal out and you look as if you're at a funeral wake.'

Lawrence jerked himself back to the present with an effort. 'Sorry, I was miles away. What were you saying?'

'What's a foonral wa- that thing you said, Grandma?' asked Katie waving her straw.

'Oh, nothing important, dear. Now eat up and then you can have your pudding. You're keeping us all waiting.'

'Bet I can guess what you're going to have,' Lawrence teased his small niece.

She finished the last mouthful. 'Bet you can't, cos I don't know yet,' she grinned back.

Lawrence took her hand and together they went to look at the dessert trolley.

Mary Lorimer sighed. 'The sooner Laurie gets married and has some children of his own — the better.'

'Well, there's no one on the horizon, is there?'

'I'm not sure — time will tell, I suppose. He's got a craving to go back to Brookhurst and that bothers me.'

Allison's eyes rounded. 'Really? You'd think he'd have had enough of that place after what happened between him and Tina — you don't suppose she's back on the scene again, do you?'

Mary shrugged. 'Who knows, he hasn't confided in me. I sincerely hope not, but we'll just have to wait and see . . . Oh good! Those two have finally decided — let's go and choose our desserts.'

7

Rhianna had a very quiet week-end, catching up on a few necessary chores and then spending time printing and enhancing the photographs she had taken at Brookhurst. She was pleased with the results. She now had a record of some of the places where her father had been as a child. After a lot of deliberation, she selected one of the photographs and began an oil painting.

She was invited out for a drink with friends on Saturday evening, but they had known Marcus too and kept bringing him into the conversation, so it wasn't that successful. She didn't wish to be reminded of her disastrous relationship. She had moved on at last, and Marcus didn't figure in her life any more.

* * *

Lawrence stood, arms folded, a broad grin on his face as he watched Rhianna handing out the pottery to a surge of children who had come to collect their items after school. Eventually, she was left with two small boys haggling over one mug.

'Were you both in the same group?' she asked.

They nodded. 'So which of you is JS?'

To Lawrence's amusement, both lads pointed at each other.

'Well, you can't both be,' she said, trying not to look at Lawrence.

'We can 'cos he's Jason Saunders and I'm Jake Smith,' one of them explained.

Rhianna bit her lip. 'I see — OK, but you don't both own this mug so where's the other one?'

Hearing the exchange, Fiona unexpectedly came to the rescue. She was standing by the gallery door, where a fraught mother was chastising her son for picking up the wrong mug. Fiona extracted it from the child and waved it at Rhianna.

'Mistaken mug identity — does this solve the problem?'

'Hopefully, but where's Tyler's?'

Fiona rummaged in one of the trays and held it up triumphantly.

'Here you go, Tyler. Problem solved — it was mixed up with the wrong group.'

Highly amused, Lawrence waited to see what would happen next.

'Well, that's lucky,' Rhianna said. 'I was just about to chop this mug in half.'

Jason and Jake gulped — eyes like saucers.

'Now these two look identical,' Rhianna said, turning the mugs this way and that. Did you both sit next to one another?'

The boys nodded. 'That's mine. It's got an orange spot on it — see.'

'So it has. Well, that's useful, isn't it? Now, if you two come again, I suggest you make your patterns different from each other's, OK?'

They nodded, fidgeted whilst she wrapped the mugs in tissue and, grabbing them, rushed outside to where their mothers, engrossed in conversation, were unaware of the minor drama.

Lawrence laughed. 'I didn't realise I was going to get some free entertainment.'

'It's all right for you,' Rhianna told him. 'You didn't have to sort it out!'

But his merriment was contagious and she joined in.

'Now we'd better find Katie's mugs. Let's hope they're safe.'

Fiona closed the gallery door and came across.

'Oh it's OK, I know where they are. I've put them out the back — out of harm's way.'

When she'd gone to find them Lawrence said, 'Right, now it's time you and I had a little chat, Rhianna.'

'What about?' she asked — all too aware that it was down to her to put things right.

'Oh, I think you know that — what on earth did I do to annoy you so much on Friday? You treated me as if I'd got the plague.'

Before she could reply, Fiona returned with the mugs.

'Rhia, can I leave you to lock up? I'm going to meet Dave at the leisure centre and I need to get changed. We can finish clearing away tomorrow.'

'Absolutely, you get off. I'll see to things here.'

Fiona stood in the doorway. 'Thanks — I owe you one. Bye, you two. Have fun!' she stood in the doorway and blew them a kiss.

Rhianna busied herself stacking the trays. 'I'm just going to take these out to the shed,' she told Lawrence.

He picked up the rest of them and followed her outside. She stacked them tidily in the shed and locked the door.

'Is Fiona always like that?' he wanted to know.

'Like what?'

'So bubbly and high spirited.'

'Mostly. She's a happy-go-lucky sort of person.'

He followed her back down the path into the gallery. She turned the key and bolted the door. When she turned round he was blocking her path.

'Rhianna — exactly what have I done? I can't put it right unless you tell me. I thought we were friends.'

'We are — it's all my fault.' Rhianna said miserably. 'When I saw you with Katie last Friday — I thought that . . . '

He frowned. 'You thought what?' Light slowly dawned. 'Wait a minute — surely you didn't think Katie was my little girl?'

She nodded, colouring slightly. 'But now Fiona's explained she's your niece and . . . '

His eyes darkened. 'And would it have been such a problem if she had been my child?'

'No — of course not. It's not that.' She hastened to assure him. 'It's just that — I thought you hadn't been upfront with me — that you'd got an ex-wife or another partner.'

'Oh, Rhia, what am I going to do with you?' he asked softly and, suddenly, she was in his arms and he was kissing her gently. He stroked her hair, traced the outline of her face. She floated away on a cloud of ecstasy.

A sudden noise from the gallery sent them hurrying in. A bespectacled, middle-aged man was wandering round.

'I'm sorry, we're closed,' Rhianna told him.

'Door was open. I spoke to your colleague the other day. She told me that a Miss Soames doesn't work here, but I've got reason to believe otherwise.'

He waved the *Brookhurst Weekly News* under their faces.

Rhianna sighed. 'My name is Rhianna Delroy. Fiona Field and I own this gallery . . . And you are?'

He ignored this. 'So you weren't the lady who was mixed up in that post office raid then?'

'I was in Brookhurst at the time, yes, but I don't wish to say anything more.'

'Right. Well, if you should change your mind- here's my card.'

He stretched out his hand. 'Les Phelps.'

He stood in the doorway for a moment. 'There is a rumour going round that you were in Brookhurst, visiting your grandmother that you'd never met before. Now, that would make a great human interest story. I suppose you wouldn't . . . '

'No, she wouldn't,' Lawrence said firmly. 'We've already had the reporters here doing a feature for the gallery and that's sufficient. Now, if you wouldn't mind leaving.'

He held open the door and locked it behind the reporter when he'd gone.

Rhianna looked ashen-faced. 'This is such a nightmare. I keep thinking I'll wake up and find it was all a dream.'

'Does that include me?'

'No, of course not,' she said unsteadily.

'Then can I take you out for a meal tomorrow evening? I saw a rather nice Italian restaurant on the way here.'

'Yes, please that would be lovely,' she breathed, her heart thumping wildly.

He stooped and kissed the tip of her nose and, unlocking the door again, disappeared into the night.

Wednesday was always a busy day for the online business. The delivery van usually arrived mid-morning. Rhianna and Fiona sorted out orders, packed them up and did some book-keeping. The business was booming, which was a good thing as, apart from the work-shops, the gallery was very quiet.

'So did you manage to sort things out with Laurie?' Fiona wanted to know, as they took a breather in the middle of the morning.

Fiona's eyes rounded when Rhianna told her about her date that evening.

'He's taking you to that new Italian place. Wow! He's got good taste. I wouldn't mind going there myself. What are you going to wear?'

Rhianna frowned. 'Haven't got a clue. I had a look through my wardrobe last night, but everything reminds me of an occasion when I went out with Marcus.'

Fiona rolled her eyes. 'Come on Rhia. You've got masses of lovely clothes. There must be something? I'd offer to come and help you sort something out, but I've got a hot date myself. Actually, I was going to ask you if you could spare me tomorrow. Dave's got some flexi time to use up and we could go up to town for the day.'

'Of course. I can't very well refuse, can I, after all the covering you've done for me recently. Look let's leave the posting until tomorrow. Then we can finish early and I'll do it first thing.'

Back home, Rhianna finally decided to wear a kingfisher blue skirt with an embroidered top. She added a matching shrug, swept her hair up into what she hoped was a sophisticated style and carefully applied her make-up.

She was ready far too early and kept peering anxiously out of the window. What if he'd changed his mind and didn't turn up? Marcus had been a dreadful time-keeper. But Lawrence was punctual. He looked incredibly handsome in dark blue trousers and jacket, a crisp white open-necked shirt beneath.

'I like the way you've done your hair,' he told her.

Rhianna smiled. 'Thanks, you scrub up well yourself.'

The Italian restaurant was superb. Over their pasta, they talked about their tastes in music, recent films they'd seen and then, inevitably, the conversation turned to art. There were a couple of things Lawrence wanted to ask her, but he wasn't sure if the time was right. In the end he decided to play things by ear.

'Would it be OK if I dropped into the gallery sometime soon? I want to run something past you and Fiona. Is there any chance of a meeting?'

Rhianna stared at him. 'That sounds mysterious. Well, I'm on my own tomorrow — would Friday or Saturday morning do — or is that too soon?'

'I can't manage Saturday — promised to do something for my mum — but Friday afternoon would be OK.'

She couldn't begin to imagine what it was he wanted to talk to them about and he didn't give her any clues. The more she got to know Lawrence the more she grew to like him. She knew there was an attraction between them and seemed powerless to prevent it.

Lawrence finished his mouthful of penne primavera. 'Great, and — when I come on Friday — d'you think I could take a look at the portrait of Anna Soames?'

'Yes, you're welcome. Perhaps you can see what all the fuss is about, because I can't and it's beginning to bug me.'

'I'll do my best. I'm curious to take a look and see if I can discover who the artist was.' Lawrence picked up the dessert menu. 'And your father didn't mention it?'

'No, I didn't even know of the portrait's existence until he'd died.'

Over dessert — luscious fruit tartlets and cream — Rhianna found herself telling him about the sketchbook her grandmother had given her.

'We're thinking of having another

exhibition of my father's work before long,' she told him. 'He was such a talented artist.'

'It's obviously in the genes. Your father and grandfather have passed it on to you.'

'You haven't seen any of my work yet,' she protested.

'No, I'm looking forward to that. How are the photographs coming on?'

'Good — even though I say it myself. I'm hoping to take some to Brookhurst soon to give to Letitia. I was going to post them, but it would be much nicer to give them to her in person.'

'She'd like that. She's thrilled that you've made contact with her.'

Rhianna smiled at him. 'And I'm pretty made up too. I thought I was all alone in the world and suddenly I discover I've got a grandmother. How amazing is that?'

He reached out and placed his hand over hers on the table. She smiled, her heart beating a wild tattoo. His eyes met hers steadily.

'It's just a pity you didn't get to know your grandfather,' he said.

She pulled her hand away abruptly. 'You're joking! I don't want to know anything about that hateful man and his rubbish paintings.'

Lawrence sighed. 'Right — I wish I could convince you that he wasn't all bad, Rhianna. Whatever happened between him and your father must have been very serious, I agree, but I have to judge Reg from the way he treated me. And — just for the record — he was a good artist.'

'Well, if the stuff at Wisteria Lodge is anything to go by, my father was ten times better than him,' she said pettishly. 'I thought the paintings were drab and totally uninspiring.'

He spread his hands. 'Well, I'll grant you they're not his best work, but in his day, his work was popular and respected. If it hadn't been for your grandfather, I would never have got off the ground as an artist.'

She stared at him. 'So how did you

get to know him — through Tina?'

'No, actually it was the other way round. I was working in a large office block in London. Reg had been commissioned to do some murals for the entrance foyer and the boardroom. I think if you could have seen them you'd have changed your mind about his work.'

'If you say so.' She slowly dissected a strawberry.

'We had a sort of unveiling ceremony. You know the sort of thing — wine and nibbles. Letitia didn't like going to London so Tina went in her place. That's how I came to meet her and Reg.'

He paused to drink some wine and Rhianna asked, 'So that was it? Love at first sight?'

He shook his head. 'No — Reg offered to take a look at my work and told me about a summer school he was running in Kent. I managed to get a place on it. He was a good teacher — helpful and constructive. He pointed me in the right direction and I'll always be grateful for that.'

He paused choosing his words carefully. 'We kept in touch and, when he had an exhibition the next time round, included some of my work. Tina was there and — inevitably — we got chatting and, well, the rest's history.'

Rhianna was silent, as she reflected that her grandfather had been prepared to help others, but not his own son. Perhaps he'd been trying to salve a guilty conscience. Her mother had told her that when she and her father were first married it had been difficult to make ends meet.

Over cappuccinos, Lawrence wished the subject of Reg Delroy had never come up. It was obvious that Rhianna was prejudiced towards her grandfather and blamed him for the family break up.

Lawrence stared into his coffee. Perhaps if he'd been in her shoes he would have reacted in the same way. He knew he was lucky coming from such a close family. He hoped that one day

Letitia would feel able to talk to Rhianna about what had happened all those years ago; even though she obviously didn't know the exact truth herself.

It was like treading on eggshells where Rhianna was concerned. He realised that he would have to go very gently. It was a pity because Reg had been a very approachable, likeable sort of guy.

Rhianna was very like him — feisty and spirited, but Lawrence could hardly tell her that. He racked his brains for a way of introducing a less controversial topic of conversation.

'Fiona was telling me you might be running some art classes,' he said, suddenly inspired.

Relieved, she got on to a safer topic and outlined their ideas.

It was quite late when they arrived back at her home. She was wondering if she ought to ask him in for another coffee, but he solved the problem for her by saying, 'I look forward to seeing you on Friday, Rhia. Thanks for this evening.'

And, leaning across, he gave her a

gentle kiss on the mouth, leaving her aching with longing.

★ ★ ★

Thursday was quiet. Rhianna loaded up her car with online orders and set off to the post office. After that, she spent a good part of the day finishing her oil painting of Brookhurst. She was pleased with the result. It showed the duck-pond with a row of cottages in the background and the church spire. A typical rural scene. She intended to give it to Letitia as a present when the exhibition was over.

She'd just decided to pack away and call it a day when the gallery phone rang.

'Am I speaking to Rhianna Soames?' came a woman's voice.

She sighed. Not that again! This was getting beyond a joke.

'No, there's no-one of that name here. This is Rhianna Delroy . . . And you are?'

163

The woman at the other end of the line ignored this and said impatiently, '*Soames, Delroy* — whatever you call yourself. I'd like to give you a word of advice. Don't interfere in matters that don't concern you. I'd leave well alone, if you know what's good for you.'

Rhianna felt cold. She took a grip on herself. 'Who are you and what do you want?' she asked, almost in a whisper. But the phone went dead.

Rhianna's hand was shaking. She made herself a coffee and taking it upstairs, packed away. The caller had withheld her number. If she phoned back again Rhianna decided she'd inform the police.

* * *

'It must have been some nutter,' Fiona said, when Rhianna told her about the incident the following morning. 'Someone who's got a grudge because we wouldn't exhibit her work. D'you remember that eccentric woman with orange hair, who got uptight because

164

we didn't go into raptures over those weird animal pictures she'd painted?'

Rhianna grinned. 'Oh, yes — bizarre cats with spectacles and giraffes with twigs for necks all in odd colours. It definitely wasn't her. I'd have recognised her voice. It was very distinctive. Anyway, it's more likely to do with Brookhurst and that newspaper article. Letitia sent me a copy and it refers to me as *Miss Soames*.'

'Well, there you go then. Best to forget it,' Fiona advised.

'Mmm — you're probably right.' Rhianna surveyed her friend who was particularly perky that morning.

'I take it you had a good time yesterday?'

Fiona's eyes held a dreamy look. 'The best. We went to that new exhibition at *Tate Modern*, had a leisurely lunch and a walk by the river. Then we went to see a romantic film . . . So what about you? How was your hot date on Wednesday night?'

'Cool,' she told Fiona, 'as in the

opposite of hot. Although, in all fairness; it was a great meal and venue and enjoyable to begin with. Unfortunately, Laurie was determined to tell me all about my grandfather and what a great guy he was.'

Fiona clapped her hand to her head. 'That obviously went down like a lead balloon! Look, don't take this the wrong way, Rhia. I know your Dad was a lovely chap and you hate the thought he might have done anything in the past to change that view, but — well, maybe he wasn't quite as perfect as you thought.'

Rhianna gasped. 'Fiona, that's a horrible thing to say. How could you!'

'Look I'm just trying to be objective — what was it my old gran said — being the devil's advocate — something like that. I mean you're bound to be biased and we both know your Dad was one of the good guys when we knew him, but neither you nor Laurie know what happened between Joe and his father to cause the rift. It was obviously something mega.'

'I won't hear a single word against my father,' Rhianna said firmly, feeling tightness in her throat.

'And obviously Laurie feels the same way about your grandfather so it looks like it's stale mate.'

Seeing her friend's expression, Fiona said, 'Come on, Rhia — you've got a lot of your Dad in you. You dig your heels in — if you think you're right. He did the same. Perhaps both Joe and your grandfather were equally to blame in some way. It's just a pity your grandmother refuses to talk about it.'

Rhianna pursed her lips. 'Perhaps she only got to know one side of the story . . . let's get on, shall we? We need to decide when we're going to change the exhibition and what's going up next. Any ideas?'

'Perhaps we ought to leave Matt's stuff up for a bit longer than a month — after all — today is *Red Letter Day!*'

Rhianna stared at her. 'Now what are you talking about?'

'That article in the local paper. Shall

I go and get us a couple of copies before they're all snapped up or will you?'

Rhianna had completely forgotten about it. She rushed over to the newsagents and purchased several copies of the local paper.

It was a good feature and Fiona was quite right. The added publicity generated a sudden spurt of interest in the gallery. People popped in and out all morning. Rhianna pinned up the article on a notice board near the door. She decided she'd send a copy to Letitia and that Laurie might like one too because there was a lovely photograph of Katie.

It wasn't until they were snatching a quick breather that she suddenly realised she'd completely forgotten to mention Lawrence's request for a meeting to Fiona.

Fiona echoed her own thoughts. 'That sounds mysterious. What on earth can he want to talk to us about?'

'I have absolutely no idea, but he's coming early afternoon so that he can take a look at that portrait of Anna Soames first of all.'

'Well, I suppose that's one up on showing him your etchings,' Fiona jested and, although it was a well-worn joke Rhianna was forced to laugh. She'd been up in the attic and taken the picture from its hiding place and placed it in the guest room all ready for Lawrence to inspect.

Anna's eyes seemed to follow her round the room and gave her the shivers. She'd studied the picture closely but couldn't see anything special about it, except that the frame had obviously come from another painting. Try as she might, she still couldn't find a signature.

She wished more than ever that her father had told her about the secret of the painting during his life-time. He obviously hadn't been able to part with it, but neither had he wanted to talk about it.

8

A steady procession of parents came into the gallery during the morning, carrying copies of the local newspaper and wanting to know if Fiona and Rhianna had seen the feature. They were all delighted with the photographs.

Around one o'clock an elated Matthew Collins rushed in.

'I don't know how to thank you guys enough for what you've done to promote my work. It's awesome!' he told them, grinning broadly.

He was just giving them both a hug when Lawrence arrived. They all stood chatting for a few minutes.

'Brilliant article,' Matt said again. 'Must dash — class at two.'

'Well, someone's happy,' Lawrence commented.

'Yes he's absolutely made up. It's

great publicity for him,' Fiona said.

'And for us too, of course.' Rhianna picked up her bag.

'I thought we'd take a look at the portrait now, whilst it's still light and then we'll come back here for the meeting around three — if that's OK, Fi.'

'Absolutely, but can you get me something to eat first to save me putting the closed sign up?'

Rhianna popped across the road to the bakers' to return, a few minutes later, with a selection of goodies. At home, she quickly put the kettle on for coffee and assembled plates and cutlery.

Lawrence was studying the paintings on the sitting-room walls when she brought the lunch in.

'Are these *all* your father's?' he wanted to know.

She set down the tray. 'Yes, apart from those two which are mine.'

'Well, you're no mean artist yourself, Rhia,' he said in admiration, as he viewed the two seascapes of Cornwall.

She felt a warm glow of pleasure that he liked them.

'We used to go to Cornwall on family holidays when I was a child and my Dad and I went down there a few years back. The place where we used to stay is still as sleepy as ever.'

He helped himself to a pasty. 'These look delicious. I was thinking — perhaps we could explore Kent a bit — take Letitia with us. Have you ever been to the Romney Marsh and Dungeness?'

She shook her head. 'I've heard of it but I've never been there. Wasn't it renowned for smuggling?'

'Certainly was. It's very lovely in a wild sort of way. So flat that you can see for miles. You either fall in love with the place or hate it. It's an attraction for artists.'

'Sounds fascinating.' She indicated the plate of sandwiches. 'Tuck in.'

Presently, she led the way upstairs and into the room where she'd put the portrait of Anna Soames. She whipped off the cover and he stood staring at it for several minutes, without saying a word, a strange expression on his face.

'What's wrong?' she asked at length.

He shook his head. 'It's just a bit of a shock, that's all. Tina is so like her mother, it's amazing. She's got her colouring and features.'

'And what about her eyes?' Rhianna wanted to know.

'No, Tina's eyes are a paler blue. I see what you mean about Anna's. They *are* penetrating.'

He picked up the painting and took it over to the window. There was silence whilst he examined it, holding it first one way and then the other.

'Do you think it's one of your father's?' he asked at length.

She shook her head. 'No, I did wonder that briefly, but I realise now; it's definitely not his style and Letitia agrees. I've got some sketches he did of Anna. They're quite different.'

Lawrence suspected who the artist of

the painting was, but needed to be sure.

'Most artists sign their work, as you well know. It adds authenticity to the painting — so it's just a question of using one's eyes to find the signature.'

'I've had a good look, but I can't find a signature anywhere,' she told him impatiently.

'Mmm, well if the artist is who I think he is then it's got to be here somewhere . . . gotcher!' he exclaimed a moment later. 'It's here practically concealed on the sleeve of Anna's dress. R.J. D. Your grandfather — Reginald Joseph Delroy.'

'Now, why doesn't that surprise me? Let me see.' She peered over his shoulder to where he was pointing.

He was still studying the portrait. 'I suspect Letitia knew that all along.'

Rhianna frowned. 'So why didn't she tell us?'

He shrugged. 'Who knows? I expect she had her reasons — wanted to know if we could suss it out for ourselves, I suppose.'

'OK, well, now that we, or rather *you* have, what does it tell us? Can you see anything about it that's so special?' she asked anxiously.

Lawrence didn't reply for a moment, keeping her on tenterhooks.

'It's actually a very fine portrait. But no, there's nothing at all. The frame is interesting though — just like you said . . . It's an antique and doesn't really go with the painting, does it?'

'That's what I thought. I suppose it belonged to another painting.'

'Perhaps it was someone other than your grandfather who had it framed. Reg was a bit of a joker. Always hid his signature.'

He was still studying the portrait. 'She was a lovely looking woman, wasn't she.'

'Yes, I suppose she was. It must have been sad for Christina — not knowing either of her parents.'

He nodded. 'But Betty and Derek Soames made up for it and, when they died, your grandparents became her guardians. She certainly didn't lack for love. There is one thing, Rhia . . . '

She looked at him questioningly.

'Now that you know your grandfather painted it, wouldn't you change your mind about his ability as an artist?'

'Well, I grant you he's better at portraits than landscapes,' she conceded, reluctantly.

Lawrence grinned. 'I suppose that's a start.'

Suddenly, she was in his arms while his lips gently brushed her throat and neck, and then, as his mouth moved onto hers in a kiss that sent her senses reeling, she entered a wonderful world where there were just the two of them and time stood still.

* * *

'Well, you two took your time,' Fiona greeted them. 'Good job you gave me some lunch or I could easily have faded away. It's been manic here. Hardly time to breathe.'

'Sorry,' Rhianna told her, avoiding her inquisitive gaze. 'Anyway, Lawrence has found a signature on that painting. The artist was my grandfather, Reginald Delroy.'

'Well, that solves that mystery. We'll close up just as soon as we can, but as you can see, we're very popular this afternoon. The article's certainly generated some interest.'

'That can't be bad,' Lawrence commented.

Parents were dropping in on their way home from school to have a word about the article or take another look round the gallery. Three signed up for Rhianna's decoupage taster session and there were several enquiries about art classes. Things were definitely looking up for the gallery.

It was another half hour before they could close up. Rhianna made some tea and grabbed the box of cakes she'd secreted at the bottom of the fridge.

'OK,' Fiona said, as they sat at one of the tables at the back of the gallery.

'The suspense is killing me, Laurie. Fire ahead!'

She helped herself to a strawberry cupcake and peeled off the case.

Lawrence settled himself more comfortably on the stool.

'Well, you can say *no*, if you like, but I had a sudden idea that might benefit us all. I like the way the pair of you work and, from what I've seen of the gallery, it's got a lot going for it — so I was wondering how you would feel about me exhibiting some of my paintings here?'

There was a surprised pause. 'Wow — that's an interesting proposition,' Fiona said, and turned to Rhianna who was looking at Lawrence as if she'd been struck dumb.

Her mind was working overtime. Was this the true reason why Lawrence had been so keen to look round the gallery and befriend them? Had he seen it as a way of promoting his own work? Fiona gave her a nudge, unable to understand why she didn't say anything.

'Rhia — what do you think?'

Rhianna pulled herself together with an effort. It would be churlish to refuse him just because she had doubts about why he'd befriended her. She tried not to think about his recent kisses. There was a lump in her throat as she replied flatly, 'Yes, why not? It's a great idea. Of course, we'd need to see some of your work. Have you brought any of it with you?'

He got to his feet. 'Absolutely, I've got half a dozen paintings in the car. I'll go and get them, shall I?'

As soon as Lawrence had left the gallery, Fiona turned to her friend in amazement.

'Whatever's the problem, Rhia? I thought you'd be made up that Laurie wants to exhibit his paintings here. You might have managed to sound enthusiastic, but you certainly don't look it — I know you only too well. If you've got reservations speak or remain silent! After all, we haven't actually got anyone new lined up for the next slot, have we?'

179

Rhianna found it difficult to put into words how she felt and had no intention of telling Fiona about the kiss which had meant a lot to her, even if it hadn't to Laurie. She was hurt to think he was playing fast and loose with her emotions.

'I'm just wondering if he's been inveigling himself into our company and taking advantage of our friendship, so that he could gain a foothold for his work,' she said slowly.

Fiona gasped. 'Rhianna, is this all to do with his friendship with your grandfather and relationship with Tina?'

Rhianna sighed heavily. 'No — yes — oh, I don't know. Everything's happening so fast. It's all topsy turvy, as Dad would have said, and I can't think straight.'

'Well, we haven't seen his work yet. It might be garbage,' Fiona said consolingly.

★   ★   ★

But it wasn't. They sat staring in admiration and delight at the beautifully executed watercolours in pastel shades, mainly of Brookhurst. It would be ridiculous to turn him away because of personal feelings. Rhianna decided to keep everything on a professional footing from now on. She mustn't let her personal feelings influence her decision in any way.

'These are lovely, Laurie,' she told him sincerely. 'About how many pictures have you got?'

'Around twenty or twenty five — if I borrowed some back that I've sold. Would that be sufficient?'

He was watching her face intently, as if anxious for her approval.

'It would fill this back wall easily,' Fiona said, relieved that Rhianna had liked what she'd seen as much as herself. 'We always do our best to promote the work of local artists. The only concern I have is that a number of your paintings are of Brookhurst and most people round here wouldn't even have heard of the place.'

'Well, that's easily remedied,' Laurie said, his face creasing into a smile. 'I've got a few more at home of Bucks and St Albans if that would qualify.'

'I don't see why not,' Rhianna told him. 'You live near enough to qualify as a local artist, but that doesn't mean that all the work has to be local too. After all, my next exhibition will be photographs and one or two paintings of Brookhurst. The only difference would be that I'm not proposing to sell them on this occasion.'

They sorted out terms and conditions and came to an arrangement about the layout of the exhibition.

When Lawrence got up to leave, he touched Rhianna's arm, 'I'll be in touch about our next trip to Brookhurst.'

She nodded. 'Right, I'll wait to hear from you then,' she said coolly and turned away to collect up the used mugs.

* * *

Lawrence rang Letitia that evening. 'I wanted to let you know that I've just seen the painting of the *Woman in Blue*.'

'Really — and did you find the signature?' she asked eagerly.

'Yes, it was well and truly hidden in a crease on the sleeve of Anna's dress. The artist was Reg, but I suspect you knew that already, didn't you, Tish?'

There was a pause. 'Yes, Laurie, I did, but I needed everyone to be sure. You see, I only had a glimpse of it and it was a very long time ago. Did you — um — did anything strike you?'

It was Lawrence's turn to hesitate. 'Well, yes, actually — look, I think we should discuss all this when I next come to Brookhurst, don't you?'

'If you say so dear — did Rhianna make any comment over her grandfather being the artist?'

'I don't think she was surprised but, Letitia, I think you need to know that she has a jaundiced view where Reg is concerned,' he told her gently.

Letitia sighed. 'It's hardly surprising, I suppose, but it's a pity because both you and I know that, in spite of his shortcomings, he was a fine man.'

'He certainly was. Anyway, I've had an idea about a way I might get Rhianna to change her opinion about his paintings. I thought I'd run it past you first . . . '

'Well, Laurie,' she said when he'd done so. 'It's a bit of a gamble, but you could always try — now, before you phone off there's something I need to tell you . . . Tina's been in touch.'

Lawrence was frankly surprised. 'Really, where is she?'

'Oh, somewhere in London. She didn't tell me exactly. Just said that she's OK and she's had a word with the police. There was no problem . . . It's such a relief to know she's all right and not in any kind of trouble.'

'Yes, of course, it must be. Is she — er — going to see you?' he asked carefully.

'Not in the near future. Apparently,

she's staying with friends.'

'So, why didn't she go to Australia?'

'Something cropped up,' Letitia said vaguely.

'I'll bet it did,' Lawrence thought grimly. That was Tina all over. She'd no doubt used Letitia's money for something else.

'I'll come to see you again soon, Tish,' he promised before ringing off.

He hoped he could persuade Rhianna to come with him to Brookhurst. He'd been a bit puzzled by the expression on her face when he'd asked her about exhibiting his paintings. Fiona had been far more enthusiastic than she had, and he wondered why.

He'd decided Rhianna was a complex person and he was going to have his work cut out to win her round. He grinned as he had a sudden vision of her lovely hair, blue eyes and trim figure. He was prepared to wait for however long it took.

★ ★ ★

185

Rhianna was kept so busy over the next few days that she didn't have any time to brood about the fact that Lawrence hadn't phoned. She'd completed her painting of Brookhurst, had begun a second, and also held a taster decoupage class which had been a great success.

On Monday morning she arrived at the gallery to find Fiona on the phone.

'Yes, you bet we will — both of us — that'd be great.' Fiona was saying. 'Oh, she's just walked in . . . Rhia, we've just been invited to Lucy's hen party. It's on Saturday — a Spa day. I've told Emma we'll both be there.'

Rhianna knew it was no use trying to wriggle out of it. So she grinned and gave the thumbs up sign.

'Yep, we're both up for it.' Fiona told Emma. 'Yes, I know you were having problems with the venue — a last minute cancellation. Well, that's great.'

'It'll be fun,' Fiona told Rhianna, when she'd rung off. 'I wondered why Emma had taken so long to organise things, but you know how laid back she is. Left it till the last minute and then everywhere was booked up.'

Rhianna had forgotten all about their friend Lucy's wedding with all that had been going on in her own life. Fortunately, it was still a month away.

★　★　★

On Saturday she was glad she'd accepted the invitation to the hen party, because it turned out to be a superb day at a luxury venue. They had the full works — massage, sauna, facial.

By the end of it, she felt totally relaxed and pampered. It was just what she'd needed after the last few months.

As they sat over dinner in the elegant restaurant one friend, Sue, who wasn't in the know, asked, 'So how're things with you and Marcus, Rhia?'

'Oh, Marcus is just a distant memory,' she replied lightly and realised that, for the first time, she could speak about him without it hurting.

Sue's hand flew to her mouth. 'Oh,

sorry — didn't realise.'

'Not to worry,' Rhianna said. 'I've moved on.' And she realised that she had.

'You should see the gorgeous hunk she's dating now,' Fiona told the group of friends and Rhianna kicked her under the table.

'I always did think Marcus was a sleaze bag,' Lucy commented. 'There I've said it now. You're much too nice a person, Rhia, for the likes of him.'

The others agreed. As they were driving home Rhianna said, 'You oughtn't to have made it sound that I'm going out with Laurie. It's early days yet and you can't count lunch with my grandmother and supper with the vicar and his wife as being dates.'

Fiona grinned. 'Well, I'd work on it if I were you. Are you forgetting that meal in the Italian restaurant? It's true what the others said, you do deserve better than Marcus. Laurie is a considerable improvement. He's a lovely guy.'

'Well, I appreciate your concern for

my love life,' Rhianna told her, 'but I'm a big girl now and I'll make my own decisions. Besides, I haven't heard from Laurie for practically a week.'

⋆ ⋆ ⋆

Just as Rhianna had decided to go to Brookhurst, with or without Laurie, he rang.

'Hi, Rhia, sorry I haven't been in touch, but I've been working in Reading for a few days. Tish has just rung me. Apparently, the local drama group in Brookhurst are putting on a performance in the village hall on Friday and Saturday night. Myra's the producer and half the proceeds are going to the church roof fund. Surprise! Surprise! Would you be interested in going on Saturday?'

Her heart beat quickened. 'Well — er — that would be good, but wouldn't there be a problem getting home afterwards?'

'Tish will put you up and I can stay with Tim and Myra. I can collect my paintings from them. So what do you say?'

'That would be great. I'll give Letitia a ring to confirm things,' she told him, her heart singing.

9

Lawrence dropped off some more of his paintings when he came to collect Rhianna on Saturday morning. They took a basket of provisions so that Letitia didn't need to think about lunch.

'My mother's made Tish one of her cherry and almond cakes. Mum knows how partial she is to that.'

It was strange to think that Lawrence's mother knew more about Rhianna's grandmother than she did. There was so much she needed to find out.

They made such good time that Lawrence stopped en route at a garden centre so that they could have coffee.

Lawrence was aware that something had happened to make Rhianna wary of him all over again. She was friendly but distant. He knew about Marcus, having had a snatched conversation with

Fiona, on the day of the pottery workshop. Well, he was prepared to wait until she took him into her confidence. Perhaps she just wasn't ready for a new relationship yet.

'We're going to put up the new exhibition next week,' she told him.

'Great I'm going to collect several more of my paintings from Brookhurst and you've got the rest.'

She used her spoon to take off the froth on her cappuccino.

'We had intended to close the gallery for a while — just concentrate on the online business but, since all the publicity, it's taken on a new lease of life.'

'You must be made up. How are the card-making classes going?'

'We don't start them properly until next week. We had a taster session and that went well.'

The awkwardness between them had eased and Rhianna was more relaxed. He wanted to ask her something else but knew he'd need to wait for the right moment. Move slowly, Laurie, he told himself. After all, only a short while ago he had decided not to have anything more to do with women. He had had his fingers well and truly burnt with Tina, and Rhianna had obviously had a bad experience too.

'Did Letitia tell you that she'd heard from Tina?' he asked casually.

Rhianna was startled. She set down her coffee cup and stared at him.

'No, where is she?'

'Apparently she didn't say exactly — staying with friends in London.'

'Right. Do you think she knows about me going to see Letitia?'

'I should think it's highly likely. It's hardly the sort of thing Tish can keep secret making contact with her grand-daughter. After all, if it hadn't been for those newspaper cuttings Tina left behind, Tish mightn't have ever tracked you down. Does it bother you?'

Rhianna considered. 'I don't think so except . . . '

'Except?' he prompted, but Rhianna didn't hear him.

She suddenly remembered the phone call and it crossed her mind that it might have been Tina warning her off her territory. Had she left the cuttings in the drawer by mistake? If she'd left Brookhurst, in her hurry, she might well have done.

Perhaps she hadn't expected Letitia to find them or she'd been convinced the older woman would do nothing about them, even if she did. After all, Tina had obviously made no attempt to find her father during all these years.

Rhianna came to with a start to find Lawrence looking at her curiously.

'What's wrong, Rhia?'

'Sorry, I've just remembered something. It's probably nothing, but . . . '

When she told him, he looked serious.

'I'd hate to think it was Tina, but we can't rule it out. She does have a jealous streak in her, but I also believe she's fond of Tish and could be a bit possessive where she's concerned. Why didn't you tell me this before?'

She brushed some biscuit crumbs from her fingers.

'Fiona and I thought it was just someone playing silly whatsits. We occasionally have that to deal with.'

Lawrence stroked his chin. 'Rhianna, promise me that if anything like that happens again, you'll let me know immediately.'

He didn't want to believe that Tina could stoop so low, but was aware she could be unscrupulous if anyone got in the way of her plans.

He shuddered as he had a sudden vivid memory of the incident at the studio. Oh, yes, Tina could be vindictive. He knew that to his cost.

'What's wrong, Laurie?' Rhianna asked, blue eyes wide with concern.

He came back to the present with a jolt.

'Absolutely nothing — just for a moment, it was as if a ghost walked over my grave.'

A ghost called *Christina Soames*? Rhianna wondered.

Letitia was delighted to see the pair of them and they sat over a leisurely lunch, filling her in with what had been going on in their lives since they'd last been in Brookhurst.

'Have you heard any more from Tina?' Lawrence wanted to know.

She shook her head. 'No, not a dicky bird. Mind you, she always was a bit naughty about keeping in touch. Just so long as I know she's OK, that's all I ask. I expect she's off having a good time somewhere.'

Using the money Letitia had given her for her trip to Australia, thought Rhianna. After lunch, she gave Letitia the photographs she'd taken on her last visit.

Letitia was delighted. 'Oh, Rhia, they're lovely. Have you seen these, Laurie?'

'No.' He peered over Letitia's shoulder and the elderly lady reminisced happily about the afternoon Rhianna had spent with her and the places they'd visited, and then Rhianna produced the painting.

'After the exhibition you can have it to keep, if you like.'

Letitia's face lit up. 'Need you ask? Oh, my goodness. What a delightful present! Look, Laurie, she's managed to get everything in. There are the duck-pond and the village green; the cottages and even the church spire.'

'She certainly has. She's captured the very essence of Brookhurst. Well done, Rhia. Tim would like to see this.'

Letitia snapped her fingers. 'I've just had a really good idea. Why don't you have an art exhibition here in Brookhurst to raise money for the church roof?'

'You sound just like Myra, Tish,' Lawrence teased. 'Actually, I think it's a very good idea. What do you say, Rhia?'

'Well, if you think anyone would be interested, why not? Although I do need to produce a few more paintings first of all.'

She felt a glow of pleasure. 'What

about you, Laurie? Would you be prepared to exhibit some of your work, too?'

'Me! Oh people have seen mine before,' he protested.

'Not for a long time,' Letitia said. 'I'm sure they'd like to see them again. Think about it.'

'I'll do that,' Lawrence promised, his eyes twinkling, and got to his feet.

'Sorry you two. Got to dash. I've agreed to help Myra with a few things at the village hall. I'll pick you up around six forty-five.'

Rhianna wondered if he'd made an excuse so that she could spend some quality time with her grandmother. He had a very considerate streak.

'Come on,' Letitia told her as she went to clear away. 'Leave that for now. I'll show you your room and then we can take a look at the one that used to be your father's. Irene's cooked a chicken and prepared some vegetables for our evening meal. She's a wonderful help and nothing is too much trouble.'

Rhianna followed her grandmother slowly up the winding stairs and along a passageway. Letitia flung open a door.

'I thought you'd like this room, dear. It always was the guest room.'

The room she showed her into was attractive; decorated in white and green with tinges of pink here and there. The furniture was old-fashioned but right for the house.

'Irene helped me to get it ready. The beds all nicely aired.'

'It's lovely, Letitia. Much more comfortable than the room I had at the pub.'

Letitia looked pleased. 'Now, I'll just show you your father's room and then I'm going to leave you alone for a bit.'

Rhianna followed her back along the passage way where she opened another door.

'It's much the same as it was all those years ago. Reg wanted me to get rid of everything, but I just couldn't bring myself to do so.'

Rhianna felt as though she'd stepped

into a time warp. There was the desk under the window, all set out with pen holder and blotter. The bookcase still had a number of books in it. She could imagine her father sitting there, pen in hand, and felt a lump in her throat.

'You are free to come in here whenever you feel like it,' Letitia told her gently as if she sensed how she was feeling.

'I'll be downstairs. Thought we'd have a cup of tea around three thirty and eat about five thirty — if that suits you. Oh, I should have said — the bathroom's just opposite your room. There's plenty of hot water and I've got my own en suite, so it's all yours.'

Left alone, Rhianna unpacked her bag and looked out of the window which looked over the back garden. It was a pretty garden, full of spring flowers. Daffodils were beginning to open and she could see a magnolia tree in tight bud.

Presently, she wandered back to the room that had once been her father's.

She went across to the desk and opening the drawers, found drawing equipment and writing materials.

The heavy mahogany wardrobe was practically empty but there were just a few clothes hanging up, which she supposed had one time belonged to her father.

It was the oddest sensation, knowing that he'd once been here in this very room. She sat at the desk as he had done all those years ago. The view from the window was of a large cedar tree, its lower branches sweeping the lawn, and she suspected he'd climbed it as a small boy.

It was a lovely room and he'd obviously wanted for nothing. She felt quite emotional and brushed a tear away.

Presently, she went downstairs and, peeping into the sitting-room, discovered her grandmother was taking a nap, Tansy stretched out beside her. She smiled and, seeking out the kitchen, washed up the lunch things and tidied away as best as she could. Everything was ready for supper as Letitia had said. She put on the kettle.

When she carried the tray into the sitting-room at around three thirty, her grandmother looked at her sleepily.

'I must have dropped off. I've had such a lovely dream. Your father was here and you, and me and your grand-father. It was May and the Wisteria was out.'

'That was nice,' Rhianna said, care-fully. 'I've had a lovely look at my father's room. He was lucky to have such a comfortable place to study. Where did he do his painting?'

Her grandmother smiled. 'Oh, wher-ever the mood took him. Sometimes up in his room or the garden. Of course, when he was at college it could have been anywhere. When his father wasn't using the studio at Lilac Cottage, he sometimes went there. It was at the bottom of the garden. Even when Laurie lived there, Reg used to use it.'

'I'd love to see it — isn't it there

anymore?' Rhianna asked curiously.

Letitia's face had a closed expression.

'No, dear. It had to be pulled down . . . Shall we have that tea?'

She set Tansy on the carpet. Rhianna got the distinct impression she didn't want to say any more about the studio and wondered why.

She poured the tea and cut two generous slices of Mrs Lorimer's cherry and almond cake.

'We won't want our dinner at this rate, but there's only fruit for dessert,' Letitia said, taking the plate Rhianna offered her.

They spent the next hour looking at more photographs Letitia had unearthed of her father when he was a young boy and teenager. Rhianna's grandfather was inevitably pictured in some of them and she was forced to admit that her father had borne a striking resemblance to him.

Lawrence picked them up promptly and took them to the village hall which was already buzzing with people. Fortunately, he'd reserved them seats.

It was a modern comedy; an extremely funny play about relationships, by a lesser known writer who lived in the area. It was an appreciative audience and the laughter was uproarious.

'Oh, I've not had such a good laugh for a long time,' Letitia said when the curtain rose for the interlude. 'Last year we had an Agatha Christie — *Murder at the Vicarage*. Myra's sense of humour, but I don't like bodies all over the place.'

Lawrence winked at Rhianna and battled his way to the refreshment hatch.

Irene and Lizzie came across to speak with them. 'It's a hoot, isn't it? Did you see the newspaper article about the post office raid, Rhianna?'

'Yes, Letitia sent me a copy. I thought it was very good.'

'I'm afraid Mavis was still feeling a bit woozy and told them your name was Rhianna Soames. I didn't realise or I'd have put them right.'

A feeling of relief shot through Rhianna. At least that explained one thing — those other phone calls must have been from the press.

Lawrence returned with a tray of tea and biscuits and Irene and Lizzie moved back to their places. A few moments later Myra bustled over to them. She was wearing a fetching red dress and looked every inch the producer.

'So how are you enjoying your first Brookhurst Am Dram production?' she asked Rhianna.

'It's brilliant. I haven't laughed so much in ages,' Rhianna told her.

Myra looked pleased. 'Of course Laurie here was a valued member of the cast for several years.'

'Really, I hadn't realised that! You're full of surprises, Laurie.'

Lawrence laughed. 'It's difficult to live in Brookhurst without Myra cajoling you to join her drama group and I thoroughly enjoyed taking part. It was enormous fun, but it's a wonderful change — sitting in the audience.'

'When first you and then Tina left the cast I thought we'd have to disband. You were both so incredibly good — especially in that play — oh, what was it called? The one where you played husband and wife . . . '

Myra trailed off, seeing Lawrence's expression.

Of course, Rhianna thought, she should have guessed that Tina Soames had been a member of the Brookhurst Players along with Lawrence.

'Well, I'd best go and chivvy my cast,' Myra said, after an awkward pause. 'Thanks for being so supportive. Now, you're all invited to Sunday lunch tomorrow. Did Letitia tell you? One o'clock sharp.' And, without waiting for a reply, she hurried away.

'There's no arguing with Myra,' Lawrence said, a twinkle in his eye.

'I wouldn't dare,' Letitia told him. 'Anyway, she's such a good cook, how could we possibly refuse?'

The second half of the play was

equally as funny as the first. At one point, Rhianna turned to Lawrence who was laughing heartily. He winked at her and placed his hand over hers. Letitia, seeing this, and pretending not to, smiled to herself.

⋆   ⋆   ⋆

The following morning was wet, which was disappointing but typical for the time of year. Lawrence collected them for church and sat with them during the service. Tim was an extremely good speaker. He got straight to the point, included everyone and related what he said to the times they lived in. Rhianna liked that.

The children sang a song at the end, after returning from their own little activity group. During coffee, several people came across to them. It was obvious that Lawrence was popular and had a number of friends in the area.

'However does Myra do it?' Rhianna asked, as they arrived at the Vicarage for lunch. 'Producing a play last night, church this morning and then cooking lunch for all of us.'

'She's very organised, dear,' Letitia told her. 'You'll see.'

Tim was still at church and Myra said, 'Now Letitia, come into the kitchen with me. The meat and potatoes have been cooking whilst we were in church — lamb today. I just need to put the veg on.

'Laurie, take everyone's coats and then come and open the wine — or there's apple juice if anyone prefers it. And then — perhaps you and Rhianna can lay the table in the dining room — the cloth's on already and you'll find everything else in the unit.'

Lawrence winked at Rhianna and did as he was bid. They set their wine glasses down and made short work of laying the table.

'Myra tested my skill at potato peeling this morning and ticked me off for leaving too many eyes in,' he told her, straightening the table mats.

Rhianna laughed and carefully folded the napkins, putting them neatly by each place setting. Lawrence pulled out a couple of chairs and they sat and drank their wine and he told her about his days with the *Brookhurst Players*.

Lunch was superb and Myra kept up a constant stream of conversation.

'Letitia tells me you've offered to put on an exhibition of your work, Rhianna,' she said now.

'Well, I — if you think.' Rhianna's cheeks were pink as everyone looked at her.

'Absolutely! Wonderful idea!' Myra enthused. 'Perhaps Laurie could exhibit some of his stuff at the same time.'

'That's what I thought,' Letitia said, smiling at him.

Lawrence capitulated. 'OK, but some folk are going to have very blank walls if I keep borrowing my paintings for exhibitions.'

The conversation moved on to the previous evening's play and the people who had taken part. Myra had them in fits of laughter as she recounted one or two funny incidents that had happened during rehearsals.

'Don't you miss it, Laurie?' Letitia asked.

'I certainly do,' he admitted. 'It was enormous fun.'

'Well, if you move back here we'll be roping you in again,' Myra told him.

'Mmm, I had a feeling you might say that,' Lawrence grinned, setting down his knife and fork. 'That was a fabulous meal, Myra.'

'Good — now, if you've all had sufficient I'll fetch the dessert. Raspberry trifle today.'

As they all helped to clear away, Rhianna intercepted a glance between Tim and Lawrence and wondered what it was all about.

'There are some paintings in my study I thought you might like to see, Rhianna. Perhaps Laurie would like to come too.'

Rhianna and Lawrence followed Tim along the hall. He pushed open the door of his study. It was a large airy room; two thirds book-lined and the rest of the wall-space covered with several colourful paintings.

They were lively pictures of everyday life: a market scene, a garden party, even a jumble sale. Rhianna immediately fell in love with them.

'So what do you think?' he asked at length.

'They're good — I really like them . . . who's the artist, Tim?'

Tim hesitated. 'Your grandfather painted them, Rhianna — Reg Delroy. He auctioned them to raise money for the church. I like art, but I can't paint for toffee so — when I saw these, I couldn't resist buying them. All Reg's best work was either sold or given away — which is why Letitia is only left with those rather nondescript landscapes. He was a very generous man.'

Rhianna sank down on a nearby chair and was silent. The two men looked at her, anxiously waiting for her to say something. She looked from one to the other and felt like bursting into tears.

After a moment or two Lawrence slipped out of the room. Rhianna covered her face with her hands and Tim put his hand gently on her shoulder and waited for her to compose herself. At last she looked up.

'My father was a good man. I don't want to believe badly of him, but everyone's intent on telling me what a great man my grandfather was too. So why did they fall out? What am I supposed to think?'

She knew she wasn't making much sense, but Tim seemed to understand.

He patted her shoulder. 'It's not up to us to pass judgement on others, my dear. I knew your grandfather briefly before he died and you knew your father for a good many years. They both had their good points and, from what I understand, they both had strong personalities.'

'Whatever happened to make them fall out must have been serious, but they're both dead now and they should be allowed to rest in peace. My advice to you would be to let it go.'

She sniffed and found a tissue. 'Yes, I'm sure you're right and I realise that my grandfather was a good artist. I've been irrational — tried to pretend his work wasn't any good, but it is — I can see that now.'

'So, for Letitia's sake, can't you try to tell her how much you've appreciated seeing these paintings?' Tim asked gently.

She nodded. 'Actually, my father had one painting of my grandfather's in his possession which I now own — *The Woman in Blue* which is a portrait of Anna Soames, but I expect Letitia and Laurie have told you about that.'

She could see from Tim's face that he hadn't a clue as to what she was talking about. She enlightened him briefly.

He looked thoughtful. 'Well, that *is* interesting. No, I'd no idea it existed. I hope I might see it sometime . . . Now, do you feel able to join the others for coffee?'

Rhianna nodded again. 'Thank you, Tim, for showing these to me. I've got a feeling it was a bit of a conspiracy between you and Laurie.'

Tim tapped his nose. 'Well, now, that would be telling, but I'm glad you've seen them. Now, feel free to chat to me about anything else that's bothering you.'

He was a thoroughly nice man, Rhianna decided as they returned to the sitting-room, and she suddenly felt much happier about the whole situation.

Presently, Lawrence collected his belongings and drove them to *Wisteria Lodge*.

Whilst Rhianna was upstairs gathering her own possessions together, Letitia said, 'So that was your plan to get Rhianna to change her opinion of Reg's paintings.'

He nodded. 'Yes, but the poor girl was quite upset. Perhaps I shouldn't have sprung it on her quite like that. I think she feels that by praising her grandfather she's being disloyal to her father in some way.'

'That's nonsense! The two of them always got on well until . . . ' She trailed off. 'Now, you were going to tell me what you noticed about the portrait of *The Woman in Blue*.'

He leant forward. 'Only that . . . ' He lowered his voice.

After he'd told her, she nodded. 'You don't miss a trick, do you Laurie? How about Rhianna, do you suppose she's had similar thoughts?'

'If she has, then she certainly hasn't voiced them to me, although perhaps she wouldn't. I mean she still doesn't know me that well.'

Letitia clasped her hands. 'Well, eventually, we must bring it all into the open. Oh dear, I was so much hoping that you'd find something out about that portrait to resolve it all.'

Rhianna came into the room at that moment and, shortly afterwards, they took their leave with promises to visit again before long.

10

On the journey home, Lawrence decided to steer clear of the subject of Reg Delroy's paintings. He didn't want to risk upsetting Rhianna again, but he hoped he'd proved his point. Her grandfather had been a very fine artist and she had needed to recognise that.

It seemed to him that all the Delroys were talented artists and that they all had artistic temperaments to match.

Instead, Rhianna and Lawrence discussed the new exhibition at the gallery and the one they hoped to have in Brookhurst and he told her a little about his work and his family.

They had an excellent journey back to Hertfordshire and, when they arrived at Rhianna's house, Lawrence off-loaded his paintings. He refused a coffee and kissed her gently goodbye.

As he breathed in the sweet perfume

of her, he ached to be even closer, but knew that before he could move forward in his relationship with her, they were both going to have to dredge up the past, which would be painful for both of them. He knew there was a possibility that their history overlapped.

'I'll ring you in the week,' he told her. 'I'm looking forward to this exhibition. Sweet dreams.'

Well, Rhianna told herself sternly, as she checked her answer phone for messages, you've only got yourself to blame. You distanced yourself from him; decided to keep your relationship on a strictly business footing, and now you don't like it because he's doing just that.

There was a lump in her throat. She knew now that she was not going to be content with a gentle kiss. The passionate kisses she'd experienced, on that one occasion recently, had stirred emotions within her that she had thought were dead forever. There was a strong chemistry between them and she didn't believe it was just physical attraction.

She didn't have the sweet dreams Lawrence had wished on her; instead she tossed and turned and eventually fell into a fitful sleep.

★　★　★

Rhianna was already hard at work the following morning, sorting out Lawrence's paintings into groups, when Fiona burst into the gallery. She grabbed Rhianna round the waist and twirled her round until she sank breathlessly onto a chair.

'What on earth was that in aid of, Fi? Have you been on the bottle?' Rhianna demanded, but then she caught sight of the coloured thread round Fiona's finger.

Her hand flew to her mouth. 'Fiona you haven't — Wow you have — you're engaged!'

Fiona was beaming. 'I certainly am — isn't it great? We went to this fantastic hotel on Saturday. Dave wined and dined me. We danced and then he proposed! We're going to choose the ring next weekend.'

Rhianna hugged her friend. 'Fi, I'm so happy for you! Congratulations!'

'Thanks. I still can't believe it. I woke up this morning and wondered if it had all been a dream. I honestly thought it'd be you who tied the knot first.'

Rhianna gave a wry smile. 'Yes, well, good job it wasn't me. It's saved breaking off the engagement. Marcus and I are history now.'

'Well, let's hope your relationship with Laurie works out.'

Rhianna didn't reply; instead she whizzed out to the small kitchenette to return with two paper cups and a bottle of lemonade.

She raised her cup. 'I propose a toast to Fi and Dave!'

'To me and Dave,' Fiona said, and they fell about laughing until Matthew Collins popped in.

'Is this a private party or can anyone

join in?' he wanted to know.

'Absolutely — I'll get another cup. We're celebrating because Fi just got engaged,' Rhianna informed him.

Fiona giggled and waved her hand in front of him. 'Fizzy pop and a twine ring.'

'Stay there!' he commanded, as Rhianna made to get him a cup.

Matt dashed out of the gallery to return, a few minutes later, with a box of cream cakes and a bottle of wine.

'Let's do this properly,' he said. 'After all, if it wasn't for you two, I'd never have had a chance to promote my work.'

After they had drunk a toast all over again, Fiona enquired, 'So were you just passing or did you want to ask us something?'

'Oh, I almost forgot in all the excitement. I'm responding to that e-mail you sent about leaving the rest of my paintings here for a bit longer.'

Rhianna gave her friend an enquiring glance and Fiona said airily, 'Oh, that

— well I had a bit of a brainwave, but I haven't had the chance to run it past Rhia yet.'

They sat round the table and Fiona said, 'I thought it was about time we had another one of those *Meet the Artists* evenings.'

Matthew looked at her blankly. 'I'm sorry, you've lost me — you'll need to explain.'

'It's what I've said. We have wine and nibbles and people drop into the gallery and look at the exhibition and get to meet the artists.'

'But they've already seen my stuff,' he protested.

Rhianna set down her glass. 'Actually, Fi, that's a brilliant idea.'

She turned to Matthew. 'As you probably know, Lawrence Lorimer is exhibiting his stuff here shortly and I've got a new display of photographs and some paintings, but we'd need more than that to warrant a good evening.'

'Oh good I knew you'd agree,' Fi said, flinging an arm round Rhianna's shoulders. 'That's what makes us such a good team. I can create a new exhibition of my sculptures — and we'll just let the crowds mingle with us.'

'You're being optimistic, aren't you, Fi?' Rhianna grinned. 'Anyway, it'd have to be soon — before everyone's already taken a look at our stuff. Actually, I've got another decoupage class this week, so we might be able to make a display of that too — drum up some more support for the classes.'

'Great,' Matthew said. 'I'll look forward to it. Keep me in the loop, girls!' And he was off with a cheery wave.

Presently, as they settled down to work again Fiona said, 'So tell me about your week-end, Rhia.'

Rhianna was studying one of Lawrence's paintings. It was of the cottage. She wondered what had happened there to make life so intolerable for Lawrence.

'Oh, it was very enjoyable for the most part.'

She told her friend what she'd done and, when she'd finished, Fiona said,

'Well, you certainly know how to live it up — a village production, lunch at the vicarage. It sounds a little ... parochial, if you'll pardon me for saying so.'

Rhianna flushed. 'Well, perhaps in comparison with what you did it was, but actually, I thoroughly enjoyed my week-end — well, most of it. Brookhurst is a lovely place and I'm warming to it.'

'Wouldn't do for me. I prefer the city. Anyway, how are you getting on with the gorgeous Laurie? Has he asked you on a proper date yet?'

'No — we're both getting to know each other. The pair of us are recovering from broken relationships and we don't want to rush into things.'

Fiona surveyed Rhianna quizzically, head on one side.

'Right — so has he even kissed you yet — properly, I mean?'

There was a slight tinge of colour in Rhianna's cheeks as she said, 'Too much information.'

'Ah, ha — he has! Don't deny it — you're blushing! Well, that has to be a start.'

Rhianna turned away and checked the computer. Suddenly, she didn't want to discuss Lawrence with Fiona, who was too perceptive by half.

'Oh, great we've got several more orders . . . Now, shall we start putting up this new exhibition this morning?'

'Have we got all Laurie's work now?'

'Yes, he fetched the rest from his home and borrowed back a few more paintings from folk in Brookhurst . . . Actually — there was something, Fi.'

'I thought so,' Fiona said triumphantly. 'I can always tell. Spit it out.'

'I've seen some more of my grandfather's paintings. They were at the vicarage and, well, they were pretty special. I have to admit I've changed my opinion of his work.'

'What were they doing at the vicarage?' Fiona demanded.

'Tim bought them at an auction for church funds. It seems my grandfather was a bit of a benefactor. Perhaps I've misjudged him.'

Fiona picked up a couple of Lawrence's paintings.

'Well, you didn't know the man, so you've got no way of knowing — other than by going on what others say ... Now, d'you want to arrange your own display of photographs?'

They worked hard, only stopping when a customer turned up and, by the end of the morning, they had created two new wall displays.

'What d'you think?' Rhianna asked.

Fiona stood looking at Rhianna's work, hands on hips.

'Oh, that's brilliant, Rhia. Well done you!'

Rhianna had put her two finished oil paintings in the centre of the display and the photographs radiated out from them. The effect was colourful and eye-catching.

'Obviously, we're going to need some hand-outs to go with them and some captions.'

'Yep, I'll get straight onto it. Now, let's see what you've been getting up to, Fi. Goodness! You have been busy! That's a wonderful display.'

'Laurie's quite a find, isn't he, Rhia?'

She nodded, unable to meet Fiona's eyes. Her friend could read her like a book. Lawrence was a truly lovely guy and she knew that she was growing dangerously fond of him.

The problem was there was still so much they didn't know about each other and, somehow, she suspected it seemed to involve Christina Soames.

'So let's have a brain-storming session about this *Meet the Artist Evening*,' Fiona said now. 'Matt's up for it and, assuming Laurie is too, when could we feasibly hold it?'

'The sooner the better. We want to keep the interest in the gallery alive. So what about one evening next week? Obviously not Wednesday — how about Friday?'

'OK — just as soon as you've spoken to Laurie and Matt about the date, we'll get cracking with some fliers.'

Fiona was in high spirits all day and Rhianna couldn't help feeling the slightest tinge of envy. She wasn't normally a jealous person, but she wondered if she would ever experience such happiness.

★ ★ ★

'I was just about to phone *you*,' Lawrence told her when she phoned him that evening. 'You go first.'

She told him about the *Meet the Artist Evening*.

'That sounds a fantastic idea,' Lawrence enthused. 'Count me in. E-mail me the details. I'll wear my best bib and tucker!'

Rhianna laughed, loving his sense of humour.

'OK, now it's your turn.'

'I was wondering — I've recently done some computer work for a large hotel near London and they've mailed me a couple of complimentary vouchers. I know it's short notice but, would you care to come with me as my guest, this Saturday, Rhia? The Silver Lake Hotel is a superb venue. We'd be guaranteed a good meal and there's dancing afterwards.'

Rhianna's heart missed a beat. There was nothing she'd like better, but she didn't want to sound too eager.

'Sounds great — what do I wear? Is it very formal?'

'Oh, it's a bit more upmarket than a roadside caff, so I suppose you need to be fairly dressy, but not too O.T.T.'

Rhianna put down the phone and flew upstairs to her wardrobe. Apart from a little black number, she hadn't anything suitable. This time, she really was going to have to buy something new.

*   *   *

Fiona's eyes widened when Rhianna told her about the invitation.

'That sounds like a proper date at last. Let's have a look at this place he's taking you to on the internet.'

She googled The Silver Lake Hotel. 'Wow — it's very upmarket, Rhia. It'll cost a fortune to eat there. Has Laurie been holding out on you, d'you think?'

Rhianna hadn't got the heart to tell her that he'd obtained two complimentary vouchers through his work. After all, he had invited her to accompany him and that was all that mattered so far as she was concerned.

'I'm going to have to get something new to wear, aren't I?'

'You certainly are. It's a good excuse to spend some money. Look, you need to get a new dress and Dave and I need to buy me a ring. How about we close early on Saturday so we can hit the shops?'

'Fine — I'll need some time to get ready.'

Rhianna found it hard to concentrate on her work that morning, day-dreaming about the coming Saturday.

Rhianna popped across to the bakers to see if they could provide refreshments for the *Meet the Artists Evening* and to leave some fliers. She then went into their friendly off-licence to ask if they could have wine on a sale or return basis, as usual, and borrow some glasses.

The decoupage class that week was a great success. The three dimensional cards were delightful and the group of five ladies and two men were more than willing to lend their handiwork for a display. The gallery was looking good.

On Saturday, Rhianna didn't have too much time to choose a dress. She had managed to fix a hair appointment for late afternoon. She had almost given up, when she found the dress of her dreams in a little boutique tucked away in a side street. It was sapphire-blue with some silver stitching, calf length and with a fairly low-cut bodice. It fitted as if it had been made for her.

At the sales assistant's suggestion, she added a shrug in silver and white.

She had her hair trimmed, washed and blow-dried and was pleased with the result. She spent a long time in the bath and dressed carefully. She kept her make-up to minimum, added silver drop-earrings and sprayed herself liberally with some French perfume Fiona had given her for her birthday.

Lawrence looked good in a silver-grey suit with a pale blue shirt and tie beneath. He stood looking at Rhianna.

'You look absolutely amazing,' he told her. 'I love what you've done to your hair and that dress matches your eyes.'

'Thanks,' she told him, her heart beating fast. 'You don't look so bad yourself.'

The Silver Lake Hotel was, as Fiona had predicted, extremely upmarket. Rhianna sank into the oyster coloured carpet in the foyer and admired the miniature fountain and exotic plants. They were shown to a table in a secluded alcove. Her heart sank when she saw the menu for it was mainly written in French.

'My French isn't very good,' Rhianna confessed.

'No problem — I'll translate.'

Rhianna chose onion soup, coquilles St Jacques villageoises, followed by a chicken dish — poulet aux haricots verts with pommes mousselines. Lawrence ordered a bottle of Merlot to accompany the meal.

They talked about recent holidays they'd been on, art exhibitions they'd visited and generally got to know one another.

'That was fantastic,' she told him, savouring the last spoonful of the tarte au citron she'd chosen for dessert.

They sat over their coffee in the opulent lounge for a long time and then he led her to the ballroom which was magnificent.

Marcus had preferred clubbing and noisy music but this was more to her taste. Lawrence was a good dancer and she loved being with him. He held her close and whirled her round the floor. She smelt the fresh scent of his cologne; felt the warmth of his body against hers, his sheer masculinity. At last they sank into chairs at the side of the dance floor, laughing and breathless.

She was suddenly aware of a hand on her shoulder and whirled round.

'Oh, I'm so sorry, from a distance you looked like . . . I thought you were Tina.'

'Tina and I have been history for over two years now,' Lawrence told the attractive, dark-haired woman rather more sharply than he intended and she coloured slightly.

'Hello Laurie — so sorry, my mistake, similar colouring.'

The man standing beside her raised his eyebrows skywards.

'Whoops — told you, you needed glasses, darling!'

Lawrence introduced the couple as Sheila and Dean Campbell — a couple of friends who used to live in Brookhurst, but Rhianna wasn't listening.

Something had suddenly sprung into her mind — something that was so improbable that she could hardly give it credence. It would explain such a lot and it was staring her in the face. She felt faint — the room spun alarmingly and a little moan escaped from her lips.

'Rhia — what's wrong?'

Lawrence's voice was coming from a long way away. He was sitting beside her, concern etched on his face. She gazed at him, as if through a haze, wondering if he could read her mind. Perhaps, he already knew what seemed so obvious to her now.

'Nothing — just a bit dizzy — so silly,' she murmured, feeling distinctly queasy.

'It's hot in here,' Sheila said. 'I'll fetch you some water.'

She returned a few minutes later with a glass. Rhianna sipped the iced water thankfully.

'Oh, dear — I'm so sorry — causing you all this problem.

'No problem at all,' Laurie told her gently. 'I'll take care of Rhia; you two go and enjoy the dancing. Nice to see you again. I'll give you a bell some time.'

They went into the foyer, which was considerably cooler, and, presently, he took her arm and led her into the bar. He had a pretty strong feeling he knew what had caused her giddy spell, but there was absolutely no way he could ask her outright — particularly not now.

It was just sheer bad luck that Sheila and Dean Campbell had chosen to come to The Silver Lake Hotel that evening. They were both more Tina's friends than his. They'd known full well that he and Tina had split up, but must have thought they were back together again.

Sheila would make short work of telling Tina of their encounter and that he had a new lady friend.

Rhianna sipped the brandy Lawrence handed her and spluttered as it hit the back of her throat.

'I feel such a fool, Laurie,' she told him. 'I've never fainted in my life but I came pretty close to it just then. So sorry.'

His eyes were full of sympathy. 'No need. As long as you're OK now — that's the main thing.'

He took her hand in his, gently encircling her wrist with his firm, strong fingers, and suddenly everything was all right again.

The evening had come to an abrupt end. After a while, she went to the cloakroom and splashed her face with cold water and tidied up and then he drove her home.

Rhianna dozed off and, when she awoke, they were outside her house. Lawrence took her key, opened the door for her and switched on the hall light.

'Are you sure you're going to be OK, Rhia? You're still very pale.'

'Absolutely. I feel fine now. It was a lovely hotel, Laurie — the meal was wonderful. Sorry if I've spoilt the evening for you.'

She sniffed as a tear trickled down her cheek. 'I was having such a great time. Don't know what came over me.'

He caught her in his arms and stroked her hair. 'You've had so much to contend with in recent weeks. It's hardly surprising you're feeling a bit off colour.'

He was reluctant to leave her. Holding her so close against him was tantalising. He could feel the soft contours of her body through her thin gown — smell her delicate scent and it was awakening feelings deep within him that he'd never thought to experience again.

His mouth sought hers and he kissed her tenderly and then more passionately and felt her respond. Her hands reached up and entwined in his rich chestnut hair.

The magnetism between them was undeniable. But now was not the right time to take their relationship to a further level. Lawrence was all too aware that Rhianna was emotionally fragile and he refused to take advantage of the situation when she was in such a vulnerable state. Using every ounce of self-control, he moved away from her.

'I'll give you a ring tomorrow — see that you're OK. But now, you must get some rest. And, Rhia?'

She looked at him, her blue eyes shining with unshed tears.

'We'll go back to the Silver Lake another time — in the summer. Would you like that?'

'Need you ask?' she whispered.

He smoothed her hair from her forehead and dropped a kiss on her brow.

'Promise me that if there's anything bothering you, you'll tell me.'

'Promise,' she murmured but, for the moment, she knew she couldn't voice the thought that was in her mind. It was as if by not saying it out loud, it couldn't be true.

11

On Sunday morning Rhianna woke with a thumping headache. It took her a little while to recall what had happened. She remembered that the evening which had started out so full of promise had ended up in disaster and she had cried herself to sleep.

Something had been whirling around in her subconscious and now it reared its ugly head to confront her again. Her colouring was the same as Anna Soames and her daughter Christina's. Could the truth be staring her in the face? Could she be related to them?

She scrambled out of bed and had a glass of water and a couple of paracetamol. After a quick shower, she felt rather better and made some toast and tea, poured some orange juice and tried to puzzle things out.

She was aware that the sadness that

engulfed her was only partly due to the knowledge that her father had deceived her. The rest was knowing that Lawrence had probably chosen to go out with her because she reminded him of Christina Soames. And then she remembered his kisses. Surely it wasn't just physical attraction on his part? Was he that good an actor?

The phone rang whilst she was tidying up.

'Hi, Rhia — just phoning to find out how you are this morning,' came Lawrence's voice, and she immediately felt better.

'Fine, thanks,' she lied. 'Thanks for looking after me last night.'

'Perhaps we overdid the dancing.'

'No — it was just so hot in that room. They must have turned the heating up too high.'

'Perhaps, well, as long as you're OK. What are you doing today?'

'Oh, just a few necessary boring chores. I might begin another painting presently. How about you?'

'I've promised to help my father replace a broken fence panel.' He laughed. 'Don't we lead exciting lives?'

After a few more minutes he rang off.

Rhianna decided not to waste the day moping. She would have liked to have phoned Letitia but realised she'd have been in church. Instead, she went upstairs to the spare room and studied the portrait of Anna Soames.

'You are the cause of all this trouble,' she said sternly. She took a long look at the portrait at Anna's penetrating blue eyes and blonde hair. Everyone said that Tina took after her mother in looks, but Rhianna's father had been equally fair and his eyes were a paler blue — more like Tina's.

Rhianna didn't want to admit it, even to herself, but she realised that there was a strong likelihood that Christina and herself might be half-sisters. A thought suddenly struck her; she even had the name, *Anna*, as part of her own name, *Rhianna*.

Letitia had made out she didn't know who had fathered Anna's child. Well, the time had come for things to be brought into the open. It was necessary for a confrontation; to clear the air once and for all.

Rhianna wondered just how much Lawrence knew. More, she suspected, than he was prepared to let on. She was beginning to wish she'd never allowed herself to get involved with all of this, because then — she wouldn't have met Lawrence Lorimer. She knew that she was more than a little in love with him.

Picking up the portrait, she stowed it away in the attic again and then settled to her painting. It was best to keep herself occupied. It saved her from brooding.

★ ★ ★

The following morning Fiona breezed into the gallery and waved her hand in front of Rhianna. 'Da-dah!'

'Wow! That's lovely, Fi,' Rhianna told her, admiring the neat, solitaire diamond ring. 'But, should you be wearing it here?'

'Oh, I'll stick it round my neck in a minute. I just couldn't wait to show it off . . . Now, come on — tell me about your date with Lawrence. What was that hotel like?'

'Fantastic — the food, the surroundings — everything about it.'

Fiona gave her friend a knowing look. 'And did he stay over?'

'No he didn't,' Rhianna said sharply; the colour staining her cheeks.

Fiona's eyes widened at her tone. 'Sorry — did you have a row?'

Rhianna sank down on one of the stools. 'Absolutely not. I'm afraid I — er — wasn't too well.'

'Too much champagne?'

Rhianna shook her head. 'Giddy spell — probably all the rushing around and rich food. Anyway, Laurie was very kind.'

'Poor you.' She stared hard at Rhianna. 'I've never known you get giddy before — must have been all the excitement.'

Rhianna was determined not to say anything further. She couldn't bear her friend to cross examine her. She didn't want to admit to her true feelings for Lawrence.

'Now, enough of that, we've got a *Meet the Artists Evening* to arrange for this Friday.'

Fiona clapped a hand to her mouth. 'Help! I'd practically forgotten about that in all the excitement . . . So what are we waiting for? Let's get cracking.'

Rhianna indicated the pile of fliers on the table.

'Well, at least we got these printed last week.'

'Mmm . . . ' Fiona was looking dreamy again and Rhianna sighed and waved some of the fliers in front of her.

'Come on, Fi. We really do need to be organised if Friday evening is going to be a success.'

'Right — well, I'm sure it will be . . . Actually, Rhia, I almost forgot to tell you. I'm having an engagement party next Saturday at the Golf Club. Dad's checked and it's available. After all, we couldn't expect to have it at my parent's place and Dave's flat is far too small.'

'Well, that's great Fi, but isn't it a bit short notice to get everyone together?'

'Oh, I've e-mailed most of the gang already and they're up for it. Laurie's invited, of course, and Matt. I'll leave you to e-mail Laurie.'

Rhianna hesitated. Her mouth felt dry. 'I'm not sure . . . Actually, Fi, I'm beginning to think he's dating me on the rebound. I think I remind him of Tina. She and I have got the same colouring.'

Fiona looked at her as if she'd gone mad.

'Are you telling me that Laurie ought to steer clear of all blue-eyed blondes for the rest of his life — just in case they remind him of Tina Soames?

Personally, I think you're being paranoid, my friend.'

'Oh, perhaps I am. I so much want to believe that he's dating me for myself, but then, something happens to make me doubt it.'

'Marcus has a lot to answer for, doesn't he?' Fiona commented. 'Just tell yourself that not all men are like him. Why can't you just enjoy yourself? Anyway, you don't have to stick together. It's my party and I want all my favourite people there — including the gorgeous Laurie.'

Rhianna suddenly felt selfish. 'Of course you do. OK, but I want to make one thing clear — I'm not into casual flings.'

Fiona raised her expressive eyes skywards. 'Pity — you need to loosen up a bit — follow your heart.'

'I prefer to follow my head as well as my heart,' Rhianna rejoined.

She knew she wanted Lawrence to be at the party; remembered those magical kisses but, the closer she got to him, the

246

more it was going to hurt if he let her go.

'I'm just going across to the bakers' to check that everything's in hand for Friday.'

There was a queue and, by the time she returned, Fiona had already e-mailed Lawrence and received a reply.

'Rhia — did you hear what I said? Laurie's accepted.'

Rhianna nodded, trying not to show how pleased she was. Her heart was thumping away — behaving like a traitor. She knew that she'd wanted him to stay over on Saturday night, but, now that she'd had time to think things through, she realised that she'd been feeling very vulnerable. She needed to be sure of his feelings for her, before their relationship developed any further.

* * *

The week was busy and Rhianna immersed herself in the gallery, trying to put any doubts to the back of her mind. After all, she told herself, another week or two would hardly make any difference when it came to finding out the truth about Christina Soames' parentage.

She had spoken to Letitia briefly on the phone, but hadn't mentioned her suspicions. Instead, she'd told her how the exhibition was progressing and about Fiona's engagement and the planned Meet the Artists Evening on Friday.

'How I wish I could be there,' Letitia had said wistfully. 'You must promise me you'll take a lot of photographs.'

'I certainly will, but you'll see most of the stuff when we bring it to Brookhurst for the exhibition there.'

'I'm looking forward to that. Come again, as soon as you can. You're always welcome — you know that, don't you, dear?'

'Of course I do,' Rhianna assured her grandmother. 'See you soon.'

★ ★ ★

All the members of Rhianna's decoupage class said they would come on Friday evening. Their display of Easter cards was delightful. Fiona had produced some realistic sheep and lambs to complement it. She was excellent at paper flowers and had crafted a number of those too.

Friday was there before they could turn round. They closed the gallery mid-afternoon in order to get things ready for the evening.

'Why do I always feel nervous on these occasions?' Fiona asked.

'No idea. I'm the same,' Rhianna told her. 'Now if we're quick, we can fly home, get a quick meal and shower and change.'

They took a last look round the gallery. Everything was ready. The displays were inspiring. Rhianna felt a thrill of excitement. It promised to be a good evening.

Rhianna had a quick supper, showered and changed into a black trouser suit with a coral blouse. She dug out an attractive bead necklace, swept back her hair and fastened it with a wooden buckle. She was just checking the effect in her wardrobe mirror, when the doorbell rang.

Lawrence was standing on the doorstep. She looked at him as if he were the last person on earth she expected to see.

'Hi — I realise I'm a bit early and the gallery was closed so thought I'd come round to yours.'

'Hi,' she returned briskly, her heart missing a beat. 'Come along in. I'm nearly ready. Have you eaten? I can make you a sandwich. We've still got about half an hour before we need to be there.'

'Oh, it's OK, I realised you'd be busy so I stopped en route, but I'd love a coffee.'

He followed her into the kitchen. 'You're looking better than when I last saw you.'

'Oh, I'm absolutely fine,' she assured him, a shade too quickly.

'Rhia, we need to talk.'

'Yes, but not this evening. Right now we both need to focus on the gallery.'

He caught her hands between his and forced her to look at him. His green eyes met hers in a searching gaze.

'Let's go to Brookhurst again soon — see Letitia. There are things that need to be said, but it concerns the three of us.'

She shook herself free, trying to remain composed, even though her pulse was racing.

'Yes, I agree about that, but we'll have to discuss it later.'

She poured him a filter coffee. 'Take it into the sitting-room. I need to finish getting ready.'

He was looking at a photograph of her parents when she entered the room.

'Your mother was a very attractive woman,' he commented. 'I can see where you get your looks from, Rhia.'

She smiled, pulse racing. 'Right — are we ready then for this bonanza?'

★　★　★

Lawrence whistled when he saw the exhibition. 'Wow! You and Fiona have done me proud. The whole place looks amazing.'

'Well, if you hadn't provided us with the paintings, there wouldn't have been an exhibition. Matt's sold quite a few of his, so we had a lot of empty wall space to fill.'

'My parents wanted to be here, but they've gone to my brother and sister-in-law's for the week-end. I said I might bring them one day next week — if that's OK?'

'Yes, of course, they'd be most welcome.'

Rhianna felt a little thrill of pleasure that he wanted to introduce her to his family.

'Ah here's Fiona and Dave.'

Fiona pounced on Lawrence and introduced him to Dave. Lawrence congratulated them both and kissed Fiona warmly on the cheek. Matthew arrived shortly afterwards with his girlfriend, Leigh, and a few minutes later the gallery seemed to be buzzing with people.

'Going well, isn't it?' Fiona said when

she and Rhianna met up briefly in the kitchenette as they replenished the plates of food.

'Fantastic! It was an inspiration. Well done, Fiona!'

'Oh, I'm not just a pretty decoration, you know. I have my uses, Rhia.'

Rhianna laughed. 'You certainly do and to prove it, you can grab these plates whilst I get some more wine. At this rate, we're going to have to send out for more!'

The decoupage group were thoroughly enjoying themselves and, during the course of the evening, a number of visitors signed up for the art course after Easter.

Half an hour before the evening was due to end and people were beginning to drift away, the gallery door opened and a very striking woman in a cherry-red coat appeared in the doorway. She was tall and elegant and her blonde hair was beautifully styled. She looked about her for a moment and then made a bee-line for Lawrence. Fiona nudged Rhianna's arm.

'Who's that?'

But Rhianna didn't reply. She could make an accurate guess as to who the woman was and watched as she kissed Lawrence full on the mouth.

Matthew joined them. 'Who's that woman draping herself all over Laurie?'

'Probably his girlfriend,' Rhianna said in a tight little voice.

Mathew looked at her open-mouthed. 'But I thought that was . . . I mean I assumed it was you.'

'Not a good idea to assume, Matt.' Rhianna told him rather sharply and he turned pink with embarrassment.

'I don't remember Laurie saying he was bringing a guest,' Fiona said. 'Come on Rhia let's go and find out who this female is.'

She virtually propelled Rhianna across the room.

'Hi, Laurie, aren't you going to introduce us to your friend?'

Lawrence's expression was unfathomable as he said, 'This is Christina Soames. Tina, these two ladies own and run the gallery. Fiona Field and . . . ' He hesitated slightly, not looking at Rhianna, 'Rhianna Delroy.'

Tina's mascaraed lashes fluttered. She extended a red-tipped hand briefly.

'So, you're Rhianna. I've heard so much about you. We meet at last. When I learnt about Laurie's little shindig, I simply had to come.'

'Yes, how exactly did you hear?' Lawrence asked coolly.

'Oh, you didn't think you could keep it a secret, did you, darling? Tish told me, of course . . . Laurie's work is quite a coup for your gallery — hope you two appreciate it.'

'Oh, we certainly know his worth,' Fiona assured her.

'Well, let's take a look at these masterpieces of yours, darling. Have you got anything new or are they all of Brookhurst?'

Tina took his arm and he led her across to his paintings. Rhianna stood stock-still, gazing after them, feeling a physical pain.

Fiona touched her arm. 'Don't let

her get to you, Rhia. It doesn't sound as if Laurie invited her. She just took it in her head to come.'

'I — I just can't work out why Letitia would have told her,' Rhianna said dully, feeling as if her heart had plummeted into her shoes.

'That's if she did — now it's been a fantastic evening up until now — so, don't let that woman put the kibosh on it. I'm going to get you a coffee. You've gone as white as a sheet — anyway, now you've met her. You were bound to one day, seeing as she's still in touch with your grandmother.'

Rhianna knew Fiona was right. Looking across the gallery she could see Lawrence standing with Tina by his side as they chatted with a couple of last minute visitors to the gallery.

Tina had tucked her arm possessively through his. Even from that distance, Rhianna was forced to admit that she was an extremely elegant, attractive woman and could quite see why she would be appealing to men.

Rhianna sighed, knowing she had been foolish to think Lawrence could have had any feelings for her. He'd merely been toying with her affections — amusing himself until Tina resurfaced.

Fiona returned with two cups of coffee. They sank thankfully onto a couple of chairs.

'And, just for the record, Rhia — Tina might have blonde hair and blue eyes — but there the resemblance ends. I don't think she looks a bit like you.'

After Tina had taken a critical look round the gallery, she came swanning across to Rhianna. Fiona had gone off to chat with someone about her sculptures.

'Laurie's so talented, don't you think?' Tina asked, perching on the edge of a stool.

'He certainly is.'

'Of course, it was Reg Delroy who taught him most of what he knows — did he tell you that?' Her voice was silky smooth.

'Something like that.' Rhianna felt trapped. Tina was fixing her with a look that made her feel distinctly uncomfortable.

Tina's ice-blue eyes narrowed. 'What exactly are you hoping to gain from befriending Letitia?'

'I'm sorry, I haven't the remotest idea of what you're talking about.'

'Oh, but I think you do. She's an old woman and she had this wild idea of being reunited with her granddaughter, but now she realises her mistake . . . It's best to leave the past alone, don't you think, before too many skeletons rattle out of the cupboard.'

Rhianna suddenly knew for certain that it had been Tina who had phoned her that evening and a tiny shiver trembled down her spine. There was something about this woman that unnerved her.

'It was you, wasn't it?' she challenged her.

Tina frowned. 'I beg your pardon — what are you talking about?'

'It was you who phoned me a while

back — trying to warn me off. Well, it won't work. My grandmother and I get on very well and I've no intention of letting you get in the way of that.'

Tina gave a short laugh. 'Indeed — I know far more about Letitia than you're ever likely to. She looked you up on a whim. Now she's satisfied her curiosity, but you're clinging onto her like a leech.'

'You're being intolerably rude,' Rhianna told her, endeavouring to keep her cool. 'This is my gallery and — if it weren't for the fact that you're Laurie's guest — I'd ask you to leave.'

Tina's eyelids flickered. 'That's fine. I'm just waiting for Laurie to finish his conversation and then we'll be off. He's giving me a lift, as my friends have gone on elsewhere. You needn't kid yourself that I'd have been here if it hadn't been for Laurie — these little dos bore me stiff . . . Oh, and there is just one other thing. I think you've got something that belongs to me.'

'I think that's highly unlikely,' Rhianna

told her, taken aback.

A tiny smile hovered at the corners of Tina Soames lips. 'Well, let me refresh your memory. I believe you have a portrait of my mother, Anna Soames, in your possession. It was painted by Reg Delroy and it's called *Portrait of a Woman in Blue*.'

'I know the picture you're referring to but what makes you think it belongs to you?' Rhianna asked, meeting her gaze steadily.

Just for a moment, Tina looked uncertain and then she said, 'My grandmother told me. Your father took it with him when he left *Wisteria Lodge*, but it belonged to my mother. It was a gift from Reg Delroy. That was the main reason why Letitia got in touch with you — to ask you to return the painting.'

Rhianna decided to make no comment about that. She thought it best not to say that Letitia had been adamant that she held onto it.

Tina looked around and saw Lawrence still chatting to one or two remaining visitors. She attracted his attention by waving her hand at him and, as she did so, Rhianna caught sight of the large emerald engagement ring on her finger, flashing as the light caught it.

Lawrence was coming towards them, but he got waylaid by an elderly gentleman. Tina took the opportunity to say,

'Lovely ring, isn't it? Laurie and I were engaged before, you know. We had a lover's tiff, but now we've resolved our differences. Letitia was made up when I told her we'd got together again. Thought I'd let you know — just in case you'd misunderstood his friendship towards you. He always was a mug for blondes.'

'Well, may you both be very happy,' Rhianna told her.

There was a triumphant look on Tina's face as she said, 'I've absolutely no doubt of that — we were before. Our relationship was idyllic.'

'What a pity it didn't stay that way,' Rhianna said tartly and moved smartly out of the way as Lawrence made to join them. She didn't want to face him, so she busied herself collecting up the empty glasses and took them into the kitchenette. When she returned to the gallery he'd gone.

'Where did you shoot off to?' Fiona asked. 'Everyone's gone now.'

'Good — I hope Laurie's taken that woman with him.'

'He was looking for you to say, goodbye. He thought it was a marvellous evening.'

Rhianna sniffed. 'I'm sure he did. Well, he's just lost my vote, bringing that dreadful woman here.'

'Yes, that was unfortunate, but I honestly don't think it was planned.'

'She's flaunting a large emerald ring and says she's back with Laurie again.'

Fiona raised her eyebrows. 'You've only got her word for that, Rhia. She was probably trying to wind you up.'

'Well, she's certainly succeeded. I was enjoying myself until she turned up,' Rhianna said bitterly.

'Perhaps you should let Laurie explain.'

Rhianna wrung out the dish cloth viciously. 'You know what, Fi? At this moment, I don't care if I never set eyes on him again.'

'Well, that's unfortunate because I've invited him to my engagement party tomorrow and I can hardly uninvite him, can I?'

12

Rhianna had a restless night and, in the end, decided to get up early and make a start on clearing up at the gallery. Fiona wasn't coming in until later that morning, as she needed to sort out things for the party.

Rhianna began washing the stack of glasses which she needed to return to the off-licence. After that, she swept the floor, wiped the surfaces and restored the gallery to its usual pristine condition. Her heart was heavy but, for Fiona's sake, she knew she had to make an effort.

When she could bring herself to do so, she would ring Letitia and tell her how the evening had gone.

Halfway through the morning, the gallery phone rang and Letitia's voice said, 'Oh, good, I was hoping you'd be there. How was the evening? I know you said you'd ring, but I couldn't wait to find out how it had gone.'

Rhianna told her briefly — not wanting to go into any detail.

'The thing is, Rhianna, I think I might have put my foot in it. You see Tina rang me again and I let it slip about Laurie's exhibition.'

'Yes, I know — she turned up last night.'

Letitia gasped audibly. 'She did? I wondered if she might take a look, but quite thought she'd come another time . . . How did you — was it all right?'

'Not really. It seems she and Laurie are back together again — did you know?'

There was a long pause.

'Are you sure, dear? Only I've already spoken with Laurie this morning and I certainly didn't get that impression from him.'

'Perhaps he didn't want to tell you right away. Tina was wearing her engagement ring last night, so I don't think there was any mistake.'

There was silence at the other end of the phone and then Letitia said, 'Describe it to me, Rhianna.'

'Emeralds and diamonds. She made a point of telling me she and Laurie had been engaged before, but, of course, I knew that already.'

'Yes, but that wasn't the ring Laurie bought for her. The ring that she was wearing belonged to her mother.'

'Really?' A glimmer of hope shot through Rhianna, to be dashed almost immediately as she remembered something. 'Then why was she wearing it on her engagement finger?'

Letitia sighed. 'Oh, I don't know, but trust me, Rhianna. Last night was the first time Laurie had set eyes on her in over two years. I'm so sorry if I caused you any problem. It just sort of slipped out about Laurie's exhibition.'

'Oh, not to worry. Tina could easily have found out by looking on the internet . . . Is she intending to visit you?' Rhianna asked casually.

'She hasn't said so. Tina is very

unpredictable. Laurie doesn't even know where she's staying.'

'That's odd. I thought he gave her a lift home last night.'

Letitia laughed. 'Is that what she told you? He gave her a lift to the station in St Alban's — went out of his way to do so.'

'Oh, perhaps I misunderstood,' Rhianna said, feeling slightly more hopeful again. 'Letitia — Tina asked me about the picture of Anna Soames. Said it belonged to her mother and that my father had taken it when he left Brookhurst.'

'I'm afraid Tina believes that to be true, because it's probably what her grandmother told her. Oh, my dear, I'm so sorry you're being faced with all this.'

'I don't like the portrait, Letitia. I don't want there to be any bad feeling and would be more than happy to give it to Tina — whether or not it was hers.'

'I wouldn't do that for the moment, Rhianna, if I were you,' Letitia advised her. 'I'd hold on to it. Keep it safe and don't say where it is. Tina can be rather impetuous. Sometimes she says things in the heat of the moment that are — well a little exaggerated.'

'Yes I see.' Rhianna decided not to say any more about the portrait.

'I took a lot of photographs of the exhibition. I'll print them out and bring them to show you next time I visit.'

It wasn't until her grandmother had rung off, that it suddenly dawned on Rhianna what she'd said about the engagement ring Tina had been wearing. Letitia had said it had belonged to Anna Soames. Who exactly had Anna been engaged to, she wondered. There was so much to think about that her head was whirling.

Rhianna took another look at Lawrence's paintings, loving the serene feeling of the landscapes. He'd encapsulated the tranquillity of Brookhurst.

She sighed. She didn't know what to believe about his relationship with Christina Soames. She desperately hoped that her grandmother was right, when she said she didn't think they were back together again. She so wanted to believe it, but somehow, she wasn't convinced.

Fiona burst into the gallery just then and Rhianna knew she'd have to stop moping and put on a cheerful face for her friend's sake.

★ ★ ★

The engagement party was in full swing. There was no sign of Laurie, and Rhianna, chatting to Lucy and her other friends, wondered if he'd decided to stay away. Her emotions were in such turmoil that she didn't know whether to be relieved or sorry.

'So where's this gorgeous hunk, Fiona's telling us you're going out with?' Lucy asked her now.

'Laurie might be gorgeous; he might be a hunk, but I'm not going out with him. We're just friends because he knows my grandmother — that's all. As for knowing where he is, I haven't got the remotest idea.'

'He's here,' said a voice behind her and a grinning Laurie came to stand beside her. Everyone laughed and she was forced to join in.

'Sorry I got held up — the traffic was horrendous.'

After a few minutes, the group moved off in search of refreshments. Lawrence took her arm.

'I thought we were more than just friends, Rhia. You and I have got some serious talking to do.'

'What more is left to be said?' she demanded, shaking off his arm impatiently. 'You've made it clear that you're back with Tina Soames and I don't go in for threesomes.'

He stared at her. 'I think you've got the wrong end of the stick . . . '

He put a casual arm about her waist and led her outside the hall into the bar which was less crowded.

'I could do with a drink and I'm sure you could.'

They took their drinks to a table in a corner. She knew she had to face up to whatever he was going to tell her and there was no escape.

'Rhianna, Tina and I parted company over two years ago. I received a very puzzling phone call from Tish — after she'd spoken with you this morning. Something to do with an engagement ring Tina was wearing.'

'I thought — that's to say that Tina led me to believe . . .'

'Rhia, I am not about to get re-engaged to Tina. She, no doubt, flogged the ring I gave her. The one she was wearing was definitely her mother's. The problem with Tina is that she loves to play games. I'm afraid to say she can be both calculating and manipulative.'

He saw the uncertainty in her eyes.

'Rhianna, you mustn't allow Tina to get to you. Looking at things from her angle for a moment, it's understandable she's going to find it difficult to get her head round the situation. After all, until recently, she was the only one in Letitia's family and now you've turned up.'

Rhianna nodded, but she found it hard to feel any sympathy for Tina.

'Now I've met her and spoken with her — I'm almost certain it was her who phoned me that time. I challenged her with it and, of course, she denied it. I'm sorry, Laurie, but just for a minute — seeing you together — I thought you were back together again.'

He sighed, wishing he could find some way of convincing her.

'Oh, Rhia — when are you going to learn to trust me? Until you do, how can our relationship progress?'

'The problem is, Laurie . . . ' She met his green gaze steadily.

'Yes?' His jade eyes had a dangerous glint in them.

'You shouldn't be such a gorgeous hunk!'

He burst out laughing and leaning across, kissed her swiftly on the mouth.

'That was to seal our friendship and more besides,' he said softly.

Rhianna kissed him back, her heart beating wildly, and he caught her hands between his. The contact was electric.

He gave her a devastating smile. 'You're looking very lovely tonight. That colour really suits you.'

She smiled back, pleased that she'd chosen to wear the silky, peach-coloured dress. It was a favourite of hers and it suddenly didn't matter that she'd bought it for a date with Marcus. Tonight she was with Lawrence.

'So, have we straightened it all out?' he asked, his fingers gently encircling her wrist.

'There is still the question of the portrait,' Rhianna told him. 'Tina feels it's hers and, in a way, I agree with her. I think I might know why my father took it when he left Brookhurst, but I don't want to go there just now.'

'No, you're dealing with far too much as it is. Tish mentioned the picture — it's something that obviously bothers her. Be patient, for a while longer, Rhia. Keep hold of it for the time being and I'm sure that in a short while we'll both learn all there is to know about it

. . . Now, shall we go and join the party?'

It was a good party and Rhianna suddenly realised she was glad she'd come.

Lawrence proved to be a very sociable person and got on well with her friends and Fiona's family. He and Dave struck up an immediate rapport. He rose to Fiona's challenge of a dance and twirled her round the floor, matching his steps to hers in a series of complicated movements — much to everyone's admiration.

'I think you've been holding out on us,' Lucy told Rhianna when she caught up with her over the refreshments. 'I've been watching you two and I can't believe you're just friends. Ah-ha you're blushing!'

'OK,' Rhianna admitted. 'We'd had a bit of a misunderstanding involving his ex-fiancée — who turned up at the exhibition yesterday. We've sorted it out, but, it's early days yet and, after Marcus, I've no intention of getting too serious, too soon, so I'm taking things very slowly.'

'Well, don't hang about too much or you'll give him the impression you're not interested and lose him,' Lucy advised. 'Why don't you bring him to my wedding next Saturday?'

'Oh, Lucy, I'm not sure . . . '

'Tell, you what — I'll ask him. Keep your fingers crossed that he's free.'

⋆ ⋆ ⋆

'Guess what,' Lawrence said presently, as he whirled Rhianna round the dance floor. 'Your friend, Lucy, has just invited me to accompany you to her wedding next Saturday.'

'She told me she was going to ask you — so can you . . . ?'

'Absolutely, if that's OK with you, Rhia?'

'I'd like that,' she told him with a delighted smile and she knew that she meant it.

The evening went by on wings, until

glancing at his watch, Lawrence said, 'Regretfully, I've got to be making a move. I've promised to collect our neighbours from the airport in the wee small hours. My father had completely forgotten he'd agreed to do it, until after he'd arranged to go to my brother's this week-end, so I've offered to step in.'

Rhianna realised what a lovely man he was — so caring and thoughtful. She wished he could have stayed, knew that every minute she spent with him was precious, but it had been a lovely evening and she hoped there would be many more.

As they parted company, he caught her in a passionate embrace that left her senses reeling.

She stood on the hall steps waving him goodbye and felt a warm glow of contentment spreading through her. She knew now, without a shadow of doubt, that she was in love with Lawrence and, suddenly, her world seemed a brighter place.

* * *

Rhianna felt a little nervous at the prospect of meeting Lawrence's parents. They had arranged to visit the gallery on Thursday morning. She needn't have worried; they were a delightful couple in their sixties. Ralph Lorimer was like an older edition of his son. Mary Lorimer was a friendly, talkative lady with neat brown hair and a warm smile.

They took a long time wandering round the gallery chatting to both Rhianna and Fiona. Rhianna could tell that they were proud of their son and had a good rapport with him.

As they sat over coffee, Rhianna felt completely at ease.

'This is just as you've described it, Laurie. I'm so glad we came,' Mary Lorimer said. 'And it's lovely to meet the pair of you. We've heard so much about you. Katie can't wait to come here again. She's told everyone at school she's got an uncle who's an artist.'

Lawrence laughed. 'Well, I must

admit I was surprised to see I'd sold a couple of paintings.'

'It's great to see you exhibiting again.' His father told him. 'You're building up quite a collection again.'

'Laurie's quite a find,' Fiona said. 'It was fortuitous for us when he came into the gallery that day.'

'We couldn't believe it when he told us Letitia had discovered she had a long lost granddaughter,' Mary Lorimer said. 'It's all very mysterious, isn't it?'

Rhianna nodded. 'So much so that we had a reporter here wanting to get a story out of it, would you believe.'

'And you've still no idea what caused your father to estrange himself from his parents?'

Lawrence shot his mother a warning glance.

'None whatsoever.' But, even as Rhianna spoke the words, she had a feeling that there might be one very good reason why he would have done just that.

'I realise Letitia knows and I'm sure

she'll tell me all in her own good time. She needed to get to know me first.'

Mary nodded, 'Yes, of course, best to take things slowly . . . Do you think you'll persuade her to come here? I'm sure she'd love to see this place.'

'I hope so, one day, but, in the meantime, I'm taking lots of photographs for her to see.'

'I love your display of Brookhurst. It's such a pretty village, isn't it? Laurie's intent on moving back there.'

'It could take some time,' Lawrence said. 'There isn't too much out there at the moment, but I'm not in any particular rush.'

'Mary's made him too comfortable at home,' Ralph joked.

Fiona collected up the empty mugs. 'Would you like to take a look upstairs? One day soon, we hope to expand, but it would mean creating more storage space elsewhere.'

'Fiona's fiancé is a carpenter and he's going to help us when the time comes. He knows lots of people in the building trade,' Rhianna explained.

They went upstairs and stood gazing about them. There wasn't a lot to see — just several rooms with original fireplaces, empty apart from a stack of cardboard boxes, art materials, easels and a couple of tables where they did their work, but there was a wonderful view from the window, overlooking the street and the church.

'This certainly has a lot of potential. It isn't a listed building, is it?' Ralph asked, studying the wooden beams.

'Fortunately, no. That would make it impossible. We don't need too much structural work doing — just a bit of modernisation to make it more viable.'

'Well, then, I don't foresee any problem. Did Lawrence tell you I'm a retired architect? If I can be of any assistance . . . '

'That's a great offer. We'll certainly call on you for advice,' Fiona told him. 'Good. Please feel free.' Ralph consulted his watch. 'We'd like to take you girls out to lunch.'

'That would be delightful,' Fiona answered for them both. 'We could close for an hour or so, couldn't we, Rhia?'

They went to a nearby pub that served traditional fare and, over lunch, Rhianna warmed to Lawrence's parents. Both she and Fiona were included fully in the conversation. Mary asked Fiona about her wedding plans and Rhianna about the exhibition they were planning to have in Brookhurst. Rhianna and Fiona also learnt a lot more about Lawrence.

'Don't give away all my secrets,' he protested at one point, when his mother relayed an amusing anecdote from when he was a teenager. He'd managed to get his foot in a bucket of wallpaper paste when his father was decorating. Fiona and Rhia laughed so much that the tears ran down their cheeks.

After coffee, Ralph Lorimer said, 'Your mother noticed a couple of interesting shops along this street, Laurie, so perhaps we could join you back at the gallery in about half an hour or so.'

'I'm glad I've got the opportunity to speak to the pair of you on your own, because I wanted to run something else by you,' Lawrence told them as they walked back to the gallery.

'I know — you've got a mate who wants to exhibit an enormous sculpture that's taking up too much space in his front room,' Fiona suggested.

Lawrence laughed. 'No, I promise you it's nothing like that — although I suppose you could say it had got something to do with space. You see I was wondering if you'd consider allowing me to work at the gallery on my paintings — when I can fit it in. It isn't really possible at home. I could pay you some rent.'

'Wow,' Rhianna said. 'An artist in residence! Well, there's certainly plenty of space upstairs, as you saw for yourself, but I'm afraid you'd have to put up with all those cardboard boxes, which are pretty much a feature, because of the online business.'

He smiled. 'Oh, I reckon I could cope with that — so is that a yes? What about you, Fiona?'

'Absolutely, we'd love to have you round the place,' Fiona told him with a grin. 'You'd add to the ambience — a bona fide artist. Of course, you'd have to look the part — wear a black beret and smock.'

'Won't you find it a bit far to travel?' Rhianna wanted to know when the laughter had subsided.

'Not if I designated one day in the week — rather than a few hours here and there. Unfortunately, it couldn't always be the same day, due to the nature of my work. Might be two days a fortnight even — if that's viable.'

They'd reached the gallery and Fiona unlocked the door.

'Oh, we'd work round it, apart from Wednesdays, which are always a bit manic because of the online business,' she told him. 'Let's take another look upstairs and decide where you'd like to have a working space. I'm afraid Rhia and I have already got our own areas, but we don't use them all of the time.'

Rhianna felt ecstatic that Lawrence wanted to work at the gallery. Her fears had abated and life had suddenly taken on a new meaning.

After a moment or two the gallery door rattled and Fiona went downstairs.

'It's probably my parents . . . Rhia, I'll have to go soon — much as I'd like to stay. I'll give you a ring to make arrangements for Saturday.'

He held her close and gave her a blissfully, satisfying kiss. They drew apart as his father called up the stairs that he was ready to leave, to avoid the heavy traffic on the way home.

Lawrence gave her a final hug. 'See you Saturday. I'll be in touch.'

She followed him back down the stairs and said her goodbyes to his parents.

Fiona turned to her the minute they'd gone.

'Aren't they nice? Well, he must be serious — bringing his parents here, and asking about a space for him to paint. I think you've fallen on your feet, my friend.'

Rhianna's eyes were shining as she replied, 'I really hope so, Fi.'

13

Lawrence was in the midst of sorting out a computer problem for a financial company, when his mobile rang. He was taken aback to discover it was Tina.

'How did you get this number?' he asked abruptly.

'Oh, I have ways and means, darling — don't be cross. Do you know what day it is today?'

'Thursday all day — so far as I'm aware.'

'Y-yes, but what else?' she prompted.

He suddenly remembered the date.

'Oh, it's your birthday. Happy birthday, Tina.'

'My friends are holding a party for me on Saturday — can you come?'

' 'fraid not, Tina. I'm going to a wedding,' he informed her; inwardly relieved that he had such a good excuse.

'Whose wedding?' she demanded, as he'd known she would do.

'No-one you know . . . I am rather busy just now.'

'Can't you find time in your busy schedule to buy me a birthday drink, darling, seeing as you've forgotten to send me a card?'

'Tina, I'm not sure that's a good idea.'

There was a slight pause. 'Actually, Laurie, there is something else. I need to talk to you about Letitia. It's a bit worrying.'

He hesitated for a moment. 'Well, just a quick drink then — tell me where to meet you and when.'

Tina smiled as she told him. It hadn't taken much persuasion on her part to arrange this meeting. Anything to do with Letitia was certain to capture his attention.

Lawrence was unhappy about meeting up with Tina, but he knew there were things they needed to discuss. The problem was one drink was likely to

287

turn into a meal, and he was anxious to avoid that.

Tina was looking extremely glamorous that evening, but Lawrence couldn't help comparing her to Rhianna who didn't need so much make-up to look a million dollars. Tina greeted him with a kiss.

'Now, I thought we might as well eat, so I've booked a table for eight o'clock.' She put a finger on his lips as he made to protest. 'Don't be tiresome, darling; it is my birthday, after all.'

'Tina, what is it you want to tell me?' he asked as they settled themselves at their table in the restaurant.

'I've told you I'm concerned about Letitia.'

'Have you been to see her?'

'No, but I've spoken with her on the phone. She wishes she'd never clapped eyes on Rhianna Delroy, I can tell you that.'

Lawrence toyed with the stem of his wine-glass. He knew that Tina was an extremely good actress and was certain she was playing a role right now.

'Strange,' he said. 'That's certainly not the impression I've got from talking with Tish. Actually, I'd have said it was completely the reverse. Remember, she was the one who got in touch with Rhianna and not the other way round.'

Tina rested her chin on her hands. 'Oh, I'm sure she did that on a whim. She wanted to see if Rhianna had the portrait — that was all.'

'What is it with you and that portrait?' he asked. 'Rhianna told me you were asking her about it.'

Her ice-blue eyes narrowed. 'Did she now? You know full well — because I've told you before — that it belongs to me. Now I know for sure that that girl has got it, I want it back.'

'Tina, I can assure you that there is nothing that special about that portrait.'

She looked startled. 'Are you telling me that you've seen it?'

'Absolutely. Rhianna showed it to me not so long ago. It's a very good portrait, I'll grant you that. Reg painted it, but I honestly don't know what all the fuss is about.'

Their starter arrived and they stopped talking and concentrated on their food. Lawrence wondered just what game Tina was playing. He felt uncomfortable.

'Well, can't you persuade Rhianna to give it to me?'

'Give me one good reason why I should?'

'Because it belonged to my mother and that girl's father took it away with him when he left Brookhurst. The Soames family lived and died in Brookhurst and that's where it belongs.'

'And that's your only reason?' he asked, giving her one of his most searching looks. 'I've never known you to be sentimental before, Tina. If you think that picture is valuable then, I can assure you, it isn't.'

'It's valuable to me, Laurie.'

Her lip trembled and he actually believed her.

'OK, so supposing Rhianna was persuaded to part with the painting, would that satisfy you?'

'It would be a start, but for Letitia's sake, it would be best if she stayed away from Brookhurst in future. You've become friendly with her. I'm sure she'd listen to you, darling.'

He finished his garlic mushrooms before asking, 'And what reason do you suggest I give her for doing so?'

'Oh, I'm sure you can think of something. Letitia is far too nice a person to tell her, herself. Remember, we're doing this for Letitia's sake. It's all been so traumatic that it's making her ill.'

Lawrence frowned. 'Are you sure you're not overstating things, Tina? After all, it's not as if Rhianna is planning to move to Brookhurst, is it?'

'How would I know? She seems to have ingratiated herself into Letitia's life.'

'If you want my frank opinion, I think you should leave well alone. Rhianna is an extremely nice girl and would never do anything to upset Tish.'

Tina's ice-blue eyes flickered. 'She's been raking up the past and that is bound to have an effect on Letitia.'

Lawrence was beginning to lose his patience.

'You know what I think, Tina? I think you've got a touch of the green-eyed monster.'

He was gratified to note her heightened colour. The waiter removed their dishes and, a few minutes later, they were served with their main course. He decided to change the subject.

'So tell me, Tina, why didn't you go to Australia?'

She raised her pencilled eyebrows. 'Oh, Letitia told you about that, did she?'

'She certainly did and that she'd paid for your fare. She also told me you'd phoned her telling her you'd arrived safely.'

Tina was examining her finger nails, which were painted with an interesting design of red and silver.

'My plans didn't work out — so I've

decided to stay in London for the time-being. I thought it was easier to allow Tish to go on thinking I was in Australia.'

Lawrence didn't believe her. 'I thought perhaps you needed to lose yourself for a while. There was a spot of trouble in Brookhurst a while back — a post office raid. Those people at the cottage were involved,' he said, watching her face closely.

'Yes, I know. The police questioned me — wanted to know why those guys were so anxious to catch up with me, but I didn't tell them.'

'They found drugs at the cottage,' Lawrence said slowly.

Tina opened her eyes wide. 'Don't look at me like that, darling! I haven't done anything bad. I'm a reformed character these days.'

She smiled. 'I made Sandra give me the money she'd made from selling those things she'd stolen from Letitia's. Dylan was furious — tried to get back at me by frightening Letitia.'

She handed Lawrence an envelope. 'Here — you can give Tish the money when you see her.'

Lawrence frowned. 'I won't ask you how you got Sandra to part with her ill-gotten gains. And I suppose that was that why Dylan and his mates were so anxious to catch up with you? They obviously thought you were at the post office when they raided it.'

Tina shrugged. 'I wouldn't know about that . . . Now, I fancy a spot of dancing, darling. How about taking me to Marco's?'

'Sorry, Tina. I've got things to do,' he told her firmly.

She pouted. 'Darling, you're becoming a bore! Never mind, I've got a backup plan. I happen to know Sheila and Dean are there tonight . . . Oh, by the way, they told me they ran into you at The Silver Lake Hotel the other week with that girl. Thought for a minute we were back together again. Strange, we're not the slightest bit alike.'

'You have the same colouring,' he said carefully.

Tina's head shot up. 'And that's where the similarity ends, Laurie. I don't wish to be associated with Rhianna Delroy in any way.'

Lawrence was taken aback at the venom in her voice.

Presently, he saw her into a taxi and heartily wished that he had refused to meet up with her that evening. Whatever had once been between them was no more than a distant memory and, some of that, was not at all pleasant. He turned his thoughts to Saturday's wedding and Rhianna and immediately felt happier.

On Friday, Rhianna received an unexpected invitation. Lawrence phoned to say that he had to work for a couple of hours on Saturday morning, as he'd thought.

'Didn't you tell me you, Fiona and Dave were planning to travel by train?'

'Yes, we thought it was the best arrangement.'

'OK — so how about I meet you all at the station and give you a lift to the church?'

After arranging a time, he then said, 'As the wedding venue is nearer to my home than yours, my parents wondered if you'd like to spend the rest of the week-end at our home?'

A little thrill of pleasure shot through her. 'Yes, please. That's a lovely idea.'

★ ★ ★

'Wow!' Fiona said when Rhianna told her. 'He must be getting serious. I didn't get to meet Dave's parents until I'd been going out with him for several months.'

Rhianna coloured slightly. 'Stop reading things into the situation, Fi.'

Fiona grinned and examined the sculpture she'd just finished critically.

'Anyway, it's a good job he's meeting us. Means you can sling your overnight bag in his car. Otherwise you might have had to put your toothbrush and

296

spare undies in the bottom of the carrier with the wedding present! You might well have forgotten and handed them over to Louise.'

Rhianna chuckled. 'Trust you to think of that! Come on Fi, we need to make a start on clearing that room for Laurie. At the moment it's full of clutter.'

$$\star \quad \star \quad \star$$

The wedding was perfect. Louise was looking radiant. Rhianna, sitting beside Lawrence, reached out for his hand, as the happy couple kissed at the end of the service. He turned and gave her a smile that melted her heart.

The reception at a nearby hotel was splendid. Rhianna was delighted that Lawrence had been able to come. He was looking devastatingly good-looking in his silver-grey suit with a crisp white shirt and a pale blue cravat. She loved the way his chestnut hair fell forward over his forehead. Their eyes met and held.

'That's a lovely outfit,' he told her. 'I haven't seen you in that colour before.'

Her dress was in a delicate mixture of green and blue with a short, green, wool jacket over the top. She'd found a small hat to match and navy shoes.

After the speeches and toasts, Louise came across to her friends with her new husband Liam.

'We're so pleased you could come, I'm having such a wonderful day and all my friends are making it extra special. When we get back from our honeymoon we must all meet up for a meal.'

'You've got a really nice set of friends,' Lawrence told her when the happy couple had moved away.

'Yes, they're a great crowd. We all get on so well together.'

Presently, they danced and, as they nestled close together, she felt sublimely happy. All too soon, they were standing outside waving as the couple reappeared before leaving on their honeymoon in the Bahamas.

Suddenly Louise threw her bouquet

in Rhianna's direction and she caught it laughingly. It was a beautiful bouquet of cream and pale pink roses and Rhianna's heart was full of joy.

Soon afterwards, they left and Lawrence drove her to Buckinghamshire. His parents welcomed her into their home, as if she were one of the family.

'What a gorgeous bouquet. I take it that was the bride's? I'll pop it in some water shall I?' Mary asked, a twinkle in her eyes.

'Yes, please but, actually, I'd like you to have it.'

Mary beamed with delight at Rhianna's gesture. After they'd had some supper, Rhianna was shown into an attractive bedroom and fell asleep almost as soon as her head touched the pillow.

The following morning, breakfast was a leisurely affair. Everyone helped to clear away and wash up, but then Mary banished Rhianna and Lawrence from the kitchen.

'Take Rhianna to see the sights. Lunch is at one thirty. Your father will lend a hand if need be, won't you, dear?'

Ralph looked up from his newspaper, nodded and winked at them.

'The sights!' Lawrence said, with a rueful grin, as he closed the front door. 'That means a brisk walk round the houses, the shopping precinct and a stroll through the park. No time for a drive if we're to be back in time for lunch!'

Rhianna smiled. She didn't care where she went, as long as it was with Lawrence. She tucked her arm through his and they set off.

'You can see why I prefer Brookhurst — this place is so residential.'

'It's quiet and very pleasant though,' she commented, looking around her at the rows of neat houses set in a landscaped environment.

They walked past the shops until they reached the small park. It was still too cold to sit about. The borders were full of daffodils that would shortly be replaced by tulips. One or two trees were already opening out into delicate pink and white blossom.

'You and I never did have that conversation,' Lawrence said suddenly.

She pretended she didn't know what he was alluding to.

'What conversation would that be?'

'Whatever it was that upset you so badly that night at The Silver Lake Hotel.'

'Oh, that — I've got a feeling you know, as well as I do, what it was about.'

He squeezed her arm. 'Why don't you just run it past me?'

She took a deep breath and didn't look at him. 'Your friend, Sheila, mistook me for Tina! Is that why you are going out with me, Laurie, because I remind you of Tina?'

There, she'd said it now. He stood stock-still in the middle of the path and stared at her, as if he couldn't believe his ears.

'You think that I — Rhia are you telling me that you believe . . . No,

301

you're mistaken! Oh Rhia, how could you think such a thing?'

He wrapped his arms about her, oblivious of the cold and passers-by, and kissed her as if he never meant to stop.

'There, have I convinced you?' he asked at last.

She buried her head against his shoulder, reached up and entwined her fingers in his chestnut hair. She loved the smell of him, the spicy tang of his cologne.

'Mmm,' she breathed, rubbing his cheek with the back of her hand. 'I think you might have done — just for the time-being.'

He clasped her hand in his, and they walked briskly back through the park stopping to admire a small fountain.

'So was that it?' he asked, looking at her with his unusual jade-green eyes.

She shook her head. 'No, but it's connected. It's difficult for me to put it into words, but I suppose I'm going to have to.'

They'd reached the precinct again and stopped outside of a small café.

'Let's go and have a hot drink to warm ourselves up,' he suggested.

It was a clean little café with metal tables and chairs. He ordered two hot chocolates and a couple of flapjacks.

'Come on; let's hear the rest of this. I think you've been keeping it to yourself for far too long and that we need to discuss it before we go to Brookhurst again.'

Their drinks arrived and, for a moment, she warmed her hands on the glass and then she said in a rush, 'Whatever caused my father to leave Brookhurst must have been very serious. Obviously, the resemblance between me and Christina is strong enough to get me mistaken for her. I truly don't want to believe this, Laurie, but, what if Tina is related to me? Both Anna Soames and my father were fair and had blue eyes.'

He nodded. 'The thought had crossed my mind and I know Letitia has wondered herself, but perhaps it would be best to leave well alone.'

'That's what Tina said but, no, I need to know the truth, Laurie. At least Letitia owes it to me, to tell me what she knows.'

He looked serious. 'And supposing you don't like what she has to tell you?'

'Well, whatever it is won't change the fact that no-one seems to know for sure who Tina's father is.'

He nodded. 'Let's go to Brookhurst next week-end — have another chat with Letitia. And, Rhia . . . '

She looked at him, her blue eyes moist.

'Whatever happened in the past is not going to make any difference to us, I promise.'

'That's all right then because I couldn't bear it if it did. Thanks for listening, Laurie, I feel better now it's out in the open.'

'Thank you for sharing it with me. I realise it can't have been easy for you, but these things happen in families — just remember that. In the past, it was so much more difficult. Nowadays, folk are far more accepting of situations.'

Rhianna knew he was right, but somehow it didn't make the knowledge any easier for her to bear. Presently, they walked back to Lawrence's home. Mary had cooked a wonderful roast dinner and the family atmosphere helped Rhianna to take her mind off things.

*   *   *

It was mid-afternoon when Lawrence drove Rhianna back to Hertfordshire. She suddenly felt a bit of an anticlimax, after the euphoria of the previous day.

'I really like your parents, Laurie. You're so lucky.'

'Yes, I appreciate that. I'm glad you stayed. It was good that you all got to know each other.'

She wondered how Mary and Ralph Lorimer had got on with Tina and if they saw any similarity between the two of them.

When they arrived at her home, Lawrence took her bag in, but before either of them could say anything, his mobile rang. Rhianna realised from the tone of the conversation that it was something serious.

'What's wrong?' she asked anxiously, as soon as he'd finished the call.

Lawrence's expression was sombre. 'A very good friend of mine has been involved in a motorbike accident. That was his wife ringing from the hospital. She sounded frantic . . . Rhia, I'm so sorry, I'll have to go. Their family live away. They're going to need my support.'

'Yes, of course. Would you like a hot drink or I could get you a flask.'

He shook his head, kissed her swiftly and made for the door. 'I'll be in touch as soon as I can,' he called over his shoulder. 'Take care. It's been a lovely week-end — sorry it had to end this way.'

14

It was Monday lunchtime before Lawrence got back to her, and then it was just a brief call to say his friend had come through the worst, but had broken his leg and had other injuries. Lawrence hoped he wouldn't need to postpone the visit to Brookhurst, and would phone again later in the week.

'He's such a considerate chap, isn't he?' Fiona remarked. 'What a wretched thing to have happened. Will you go on your own — if he can't make it?'

'I'm not sure,' Rhianna told her. 'I want to see my grandmother again, but I'd rather have gone with Laurie . . . Now, have we got enough materials for the Art and Craft class on Friday?'

Fiona had already left when the gallery phone rang. Rhianna recognised the voice at once. It was Tina Soames.

'Hallo Rhianna — I was wondering if

you'd had any more thoughts about handing back my mother's portrait,' she said without preamble.

'Not really. I'm afraid I've been too busy in other directions. There's no rush, is there?' Rhianna asked, playing for time.

'I would appreciate it if you'd let me take a look at it. I could come to the gallery.'

'I'm afraid that isn't convenient this week,' Rhianna said firmly. 'I'll let you know when would be a good time, if you'll give me your number.'

'Oh, that won't be necessary, I'll keep in touch or you can give Laurie a message for me. We had such a lovely evening last Thursday, did he mention it? It was my birthday and he took me out to dinner.'

Before Rhianna could reply the phone went dead and she was left feeling utterly confused and miserable.

★　★　★

'Of course you can come and stay,' Letitia told Rhianna when she phoned her later that evening. 'Is Laurie coming too?'

'No, I shouldn't think so,' Rhianna said dully.

'That sounded rather definite, dear — any particular reason?'

'Two,' Rhianna told her, realising she couldn't keep anything from her grandmother.

She told her about Lawrence's friend's accident. Letitia sympathised.

'And the second reason? I suspect that has something to do with you, Rhianna.'

'I told Lawrence I wasn't prepared to be in a relationship with three in it! I really thought his affair with Tina was over, but he took her out to dinner last week.'

'Ah, it was her birthday,' Letitia said. 'Did he tell you?'

'No, *she* did. It's obvious he's still got feelings for her.'

Letitia sighed. 'Have you challenged him about it?'

'No. I'm finding the whole thing humiliating. We'd had such a lovely week-end, too.'

'Well, if I were you dear, I'd wait until you've spoken to Laurie. There could be a perfectly innocent explanation. I'm afraid Tina can be very persuasive. She can also be melodramatic. Perhaps Laurie thought she was at low ebb. I think she's been finding this situation with you and me a bit difficult.'

'But she was the one who left all the information lying in the drawer for you to find,' Rhianna pointed out.

'Yes, but I'm beginning to think that was a mistake. She did leave in rather a hurry. Anyway, you come to me for the week-end and we'll have a nice time and try to forget all this. I'm sure Laurie wouldn't intentionally hurt you. He's far too nice a person for that.'

Putting the phone down, Rhianna sat with her head in her hands for several minutes. That was the problem, wasn't it? Lawrence was nice to everyone, including Tina. Why couldn't he have told her he'd taken Tina out to dinner on her birthday? Why let Rhianna believe his relationship with his ex-fiancée was over?

★   ★   ★

The rest of the week passed without incident. The first Art and Craft class on Friday was great fun, although the standard was varied. They had ten students. Some worked with Fiona, trying their hand at sculpture; whilst those who were with Rhianna, used pastels to produce still life pictures.

That evening, Rhianna received a short e-mail from Lawrence, saying he thought he might have to postpone the trip.

Rhianna was getting used to the journey to Brookhurst now and arrived before lunch on Saturday. In the boot of her car was Anna Soames' portrait.

She was sitting drinking tea with Letitia when the doorbell rang. She opened it to find Lawrence standing on the step.

'Sorry I haven't phoned, but I honestly didn't know if I'd make it or not — so I decided to surprise the pair of you.'

Rhianna fixed him with a cold stare. 'You're full of surprises, aren't you?'

Lawrence had been primed by Letitia and knew that he had a delicate situation to sort out yet again.

'There are things I urgently need to explain. But, before I do, we need to sort out this business about Anna Soames once and for all, don't you think?'

Seeing her expression he added, 'Yes, I've spoken with Tish. Told her if I didn't get here by three o'clock, I wouldn't be able to make it today. It's now a quarter past, so she must have given me up.'

Rhianna's blue eyes flashed with anger. 'Right — and did you also tell her you'd been wining and dining Tina?'

He swallowed. 'You'd already told her that. Look, I know I should have told you, but last week-end was so special that I didn't want to spoil it. I know I need to explain but, please Rhia, can we put it on hold, for just a little while longer?'

She capitulated. 'OK, I'm prepared to put our differences aside for Letitia's sake.'

They went into the sitting-room. Rhianna thought her grandmother looked relieved to see him, and wondered what had been said on the phone.

After Lawrence had polished off several sandwiches and drunk two cups of tea, Letitia set Tansy on the carpet and said, 'My dears, I think it's high time I told you what happened between Reg and Joe all those years ago. The misunderstandings that have arisen, due to all this, have been unbearable. I've tried to protect Tina, but only seem to have made matters worse.'

Rhianna clasped her hands. 'This is to do with the identity of Tina's father, isn't it? You said you didn't know who he was. Were you just continuing to be economical with the truth?'

'No, Rhianna. I genuinely don't know but, as you've surmised, it's what the falling out was about and it was a very great falling out.'

'Take your time, Tish. Don't distress yourself,' Lawrence urged.

Letitia suddenly looked very small and frail. 'You need to know, Rhianna, that before he met your mother, your father was engaged to Anna Soames.'

Rhianna gasped. This was unexpected.

'And, I suppose my grandfather disapproved?'

'Oh, yes and so did I. They were both so young — but then, when we realised how serious they were, we came round to the idea.'

'And then . . . ?' Rhianna prompted gently.

'Anna asked Reg to paint her portrait, as a wedding gift for Joe.'

Suddenly Rhianna had a premonition of what was coming next. Letitia was twisting her paper napkin round and round in her lap. She said in a rush, 'Anna was a very lovely woman. Unfortunately, she was also very flighty. Reg was — was besotted with her and I'm afraid temptation got the better of him.'

Rhianna clapped her hand to her mouth as her suspicions were confirmed.

'Are you telling me that my grandfather and Anna . . . ?'

Letitia lowered her eyes. 'Yes, they had a brief affair. Joe was away, working in London at that time. When Anna became pregnant, he was convinced that the baby wasn't his — couldn't have been. And then, somehow, he found out that she and your grandfather had been lovers.'

Rhianna was appalled. 'And that's what the row was about? No wonder my father left — that's perfectly horrid!'

Letitia nodded. 'Yes, he had every right to be furious with your grandfather. Eventually, when it was too late,

Anna confessed to her mother that Joe wasn't the child's father. She gave her word to Reg that she wouldn't give him away, but she also told him that she didn't believe either he or Joe was the father of her child. Anna went to her grave without divulging the name. At that time, I couldn't track Joe down, although I tried — believe you me.'

'So you and Reg tried to make amends by bringing up Tina when her grandparents had both died?' Lawrence said.

Letitia nodded. There was silence for a few moments and then she said, just as if they'd been discussing the weather, 'Well, all this talking has made me thirsty. Let's have some more tea and, this time, I've actually managed to cook a cake myself. Irene helped me get it in and out of the oven.'

Stunned by what she'd just heard, Rhianna followed Lawrence into the kitchen.

'That's a bit of a turn out for the books, as Dad would say,' Lawrence remarked as he filled the kettle.

'It's all so very sad. Why would Anna fling everything away like that — just for a sordid affair?'

Lawrence picked up a plate. 'Maybe it was just that she was so young and wasn't ready for marriage. I'm afraid we'll never know . . . Where's this cake — ah, hiding under that cloth.'

'Wow that looks good . . . Laurie, I've brought the portrait with me of *The Woman in Blue*.'

He stared at her. 'You've brought it here? But I thought we'd all agreed that you'd hang on to it.'

'I know but after Tina phoned me, I thought it might be best. She wanted to come to the gallery in the week to see the portrait. I told her, *no*. She seems to be getting a bit obsessive.'

'Yes, I don't disagree there.'

He carried the loaded tea-tray into the sitting-room. They lightened the conversation by telling Letitia more about the wedding the previous week-end and then Lawrence told them how

317

his friend was progressing after his accident.

'Rhia and Fiona have consented to me renting some space at the gallery to do some painting; although there are a few things I need to put right with Rhia first or she might decide to withdraw her offer.'

'Such as why you took Tina out to dinner on her birthday?' Letitia suggested, giving him an old fashioned look. 'That wasn't exactly one of your better ideas, was it, Laurie?'

'Actually, it wasn't my idea,' Lawrence said. 'It was a fait accompli. Anyway, enough of that for the moment . . . This cake is absolutely delicious.'

'I think that means he wants another slice,' Letitia teased.

After a while, Rhianna went to fetch the portrait, refusing Lawrence's offer of help. She felt a great sense of relief, now that she'd learnt her father wasn't Christina Soames' father, too. But, she couldn't help feeling disloyal to his memory — knowing she ought never to have doubted him in the first place.

She lugged the portrait into the sitting room and whipped off the cloth that was covering it. Letitia's eyes widened.

'My goodness. I'd forgotten how big it was. She was certainly a looker, wasn't she? You've got to admit that.'

'I suppose so,' Rhianna said ungraciously. 'We've both looked at this over and over and can't find anything special about it. I'm not sure quite what Tina expects, but I honestly think she should have the wretched thing, if she's so passionate about it.'

Letitia was fingering the frame. 'Tina is convinced that somehow this portrait holds the clue as to who her father was — and more besides. It was something her grandmother said to her. Of course, we'd no idea if your father still had it in his possession.'

Lawrence picked up the portrait. 'As Rhia says, we've examined it thoroughly and can't find anything other than that one set of initials which are just here — look.'

Letitia peered closely. 'Oh, yes, Reg certainly hid them well, didn't he?'

She looked thoughtful and suddenly clicked her fingers.

'I suppose — have either of you attempted to remove the frame?'

Rhianna stared at her. 'No, although, perhaps my father did. I mean it isn't the right frame for the picture, is it? I wonder where it came from?'

'I know the answer to that one, but let's take a look first.'

'It's going to make a bit of a mess,' Lawrence told her, laying the portrait on the floor.

'There's a pocket knife in that drawer.'

Rhianna got up to fetch it and they watched with bated breath as Lawrence carefully cut round the edge of the frame. After a few minutes, he looked up. 'Can you slide your hand inside, Rhia? It's smaller than mine.'

At first she found nothing and then she said, 'There's something here, but I can't quite get hold of it.'

Letitia handed her a letter opener. It took a little manoeuvring to retrieve the envelope from its hiding place. Rhianna handed it to Letitia who, in turn, gave it to Lawrence.

'It's a letter from Anna Soames to her unborn child.'

'Read it, Laurie, if you will,' Letitia asked him.

'*To my darling child.*

One day, when I am no longer on this earth, you will find out the truth. Joe Delroy was a good man — the best — but he was not your father and nor was Reg. The truth is, I was deeply in love with another man, who will never learn of your existence from me.

We could not marry because, when we met, both of us were engaged to someone else and it would have wrecked too many lives. His name was Henry Parsons.

Your loving mother,
Anna Soames.'

Rhianna gasped. 'Uncle Henry, but he and his wife, Penny, never had any children. He ought to be told he has a daughter.'

Letitia was shaking her head in disbelief. 'All these years — all this heartache. If only Anna had told us the truth.'

'Perhaps she didn't think it was a good idea at the time,' Lawrence said. 'I mean, she couldn't have known how things would turn out.'

Letitia's eyes misted. 'Poor Tina, all these years never knowing who her father was. There was gossip, you know. Children can be cruel.'

Rhianna was fishing about inside the cavity between the canvas and the frame.

'Wait a minute — there's another envelope!'

This was even more difficult to retrieve than the first one. It was flat and contained a thick sheet of discoloured paper covered with copperplate writing.

Her eyes widened. 'Is this what I think it is?'

'Good gracious — it's the original title deeds to *Lilac Cottage*. I hunted high and low for these when Reg died. I knew it would cause a problem, if I ever wanted to sell up, but his will clearly stated that, apart from one or two minor bequests, he'd left everything to me. I don't understand what this means.'

A sheet of paper fluttered to the floor and Lawrence picked it up. He handed it to Letitia who scanned it.

'It appears that Reg left the cottage to Anna and her offspring. Anna put the deeds in here for safe-keeping. No wonder it's caused so much grief over the years. Betty Soames must have known there was something of importance hidden in the picture frame, but she didn't breathe a word.'

'Perhaps she didn't know what it was Anna had hidden. I suppose she must have done it after she broke up with your son,' Lawrence said.

'Yes — the portrait would have been in the studio at the cottage. Joe would have found it when he was collecting his other things.'

'Did he know she'd been planning to give it to him as a wedding present?'

Letitia shook her head. 'We'll never know, Rhianna. But it was Anna's father, Derek, who had it framed. He bought the frame in a house sale. Obviously, Reg had a fit of conscience and left Anna the title deeds. We'd often discussed making the cottage over to the Soames, but never got round to it . . . Well, Tina will be pleased.'

'I'm afraid, I can't get in touch with her,' Lawrence said. 'I'll have to wait for her to contact me.'

'I suppose Reg would have put it all in his new will, but you see, he never got round to updating it.'

'So it's actually up to you what you choose to do about this?' Rhianna enquired.

Letitia nodded. 'I intend to follow Reg's wishes and let Tina have the cottage now — sooner rather than later. I must contact my solicitor . . . Now, haven't you two got some things to sort out? Then, I thought we'd all go out for supper at The White Unicorn. Their new kitchen is installed and I understand the food is good.'

Rhianna and Lawrence went into the kitchen which was warm and cosy. She listened as he told her why he'd had dinner with Christina Soames. He also filled her in with a great deal more.

'So you see Tina is — how shall I put it — emotionally fragile. Over the years she's mixed with the wrong sort of people — got heavily into debt at one time. Her so-called friends got her into bad habits, soft drugs, drink, and encouraged her to lead an extravagant lifestyle. When I met her, I didn't know any of this to begin with. She was bewitching — like her mother — but she soon showed herself in her true colours.

'When we parted company she set fire to the studio and a quantity of my paintings went up in smoke.'

Rhianna found it difficult to credit what he was telling her.

'Can you forgive me, Rhia, for being so gullible? It wasn't love, I realise that now; it was infatuation.'

She went into his outstretched arms and he kissed her passionately.

'One day soon I'll show you just how much I love you,' he told her.

'I'll hold you to that,' she said with a smile, 'if ever we get the chance to be on our own for any length of time.'

She reached up and traced the outline of his face.

'Shall we be making tracks?' Letitia called from the hallway.

'Coming,' Lawrence called back and they stifled their laughter.

* * *

Tina Soames had taken one look at the portrait of her mother and declared she couldn't possibly accommodate it. Letitia arranged to gift her the cottage because of the legal complications, but

Tina didn't want that either and said she would sell it.

★   ★   ★

The exhibition of Rhianna and Lawrence's paintings took place on a fine May day. It was a great success and, much to Tim and Myra's delight, they raised a lot of money for the church roof fund. Everyone came to support them — Fiona and Dave, Lawrence's family and, of course, Letitia.

That evening, Lawrence took Rhianna on a short drive.

'It's a mystery tour,' he explained.

He pulled up outside *Lilac Cottage*. It was looking particularly lovely that evening.

'You've never got this place out of your system, have you, Laurie?'

He shook his head. 'I thought I could never live here again, but I've changed my mind. Tina was in a hurry to sell because she's going to New Zealand to visit Henry Parsons and so — I've bought it off her.'

Rhianna gasped. 'You've done what?'

'You see, I made a fair bit of money in the States and inherited a bit more from my grandfather. My parents have helped make up the deficit.'

'You're going to move to Brookhurst? But what about us — the gallery?'

His green eyes sparkled. 'Oh, that's the good bit. I thought we could have this place as our week-end home. That way we'd get to see Letitia, Tim and Myra and all our other friends — and for the rest of the week — we could live at yours.'

She stared at him uncomprehendingly for a moment. He took her by the hand and led her into the garden where the lilac tree was in full bloom.

'What I thought was, Rhia . . . '

'Yes?' she prompted, her heart pounding.

'How would it be if we got married in Brookhurst church?'

After a moment Rhianna said, 'How would it be if you asked me first?'

For an answer, he took her in his arms and whispered against her hair, 'Rhianna Delroy. I love you deeply and want you to be my wife. Will you marry me?'

'Yes — oh, yes, please,' she breathed, blue eyes shining.

There was a resounding cheer from the direction of the garden gate as he kissed her.

Looking up, they saw a sea of grinning faces.

'Aunty Tish said you'd be here . . . If you're getting married, can I be a bridesmaid?' asked Katie.

Rhia bent down to the little girl's level.

'You certainly can, because you've just given me such a good idea.'

She walked to Letitia's side and threw an arm about the elderly lady's shoulder.

'How would it be if I called you Grandma Tish?'

Letitia Delroy beamed. 'That would be just fine, my darling granddaughter.'

We do hope that you have enjoyed reading this large print book.

Did you know that all of our titles are available for purchase?

We publish a wide range of high quality large print books including:
Romances, Mysteries, Classics
General Fiction
Non Fiction and Westerns

Special interest titles available in large print are:
The Little Oxford Dictionary
Music Book, Song Book
Hymn Book, Service Book

Also available from us courtesy of Oxford University Press:
Young Readers' Dictionary
(large print edition)
Young Readers' Thesaurus
(large print edition)

For further information or a free brochure, please contact us at:
Ulverscroft Large Print Books Ltd.,
The Green, Bradgate Road, Anstey,
Leicester, LE7 7FU, England.
Tel: (00 44) **0116 236 4325**
Fax: (00 44) **0116 234 0205**